TRICYCLIST

JOON OLUCHI LEE

TRICYCLIST

NIGHTBOAT BOOKS
NEW YORK

Printed in the United States

ISBN: 978-1-64362-325-2

Design and composition by Kit Schluter
Typeset in LTC Goudy Oldstyle Pro

Cover art: *Self, Verso* by Kye Christensen-Knowles
Courtesy of the artist and LOMEX Gallery

Cataloging-in-publication data is available
from the Library of Congress

Nightboat Books
New York
www.nightboat.org

To the young men leaving the village that year, he gave a shield, or a knife, or a bow. To the young women, determined to seek their own living, he gave a falcon, or a dog, or ring.

—Jeanette Winterson,
Oranges Are Not the Only Fruit

0o0

FEI FEI, JEAN, AND I WERE AT AN ESTATE SALE UP IN Healdsburg. We were three Asian-Americans hanging about in a small cutesy town dotted with wide-hipped houses owned by mostly white, mostly old, mostly very rich people. Fei Fei owns a vintage clothing boutique in San Francisco, and Jean and I were tagging along on one of her buying jags. Some old queen who's a friend of Jean's who's an assistant director at a big auction house called up Fei Fei last week to let her know about a famous figure skater from the 1970s who had died: all her fabulous stuff was going to be liquidated. Fei Fei and I were surprised at first that there was a famous figure skater from California, but Jean informed us that in fact, Northern California has quite the tradition in figure skating. Fei Fei didn't know too much about figure skating, nor did I, and as it turned out, neither did Jean. We looked the skater up on the Internet and found out she was not really all that famous: she came in third at the National Championships in the mid-'70s, and 21st the same year at the World Championships. To us that didn't sound like it would make her famous, but we looked at her pictures and agreed she was gorgeous. Her costumes looked future-oriented, anachronistic, full of holes that were extravagantly blinged out in shimmers and embroidery, freeing and baring fragile body parts like wrists, neck, and groin, compared to the demure and matte dresses of her competitors. So we figured she must have left behind a lot of beautiful, if not expensive, designer clothes. And she was Asian-American, which made us feel endeared to her.

The estate sale wasn't really a sale; it was more like if you took an auction catalogue and adapted it for the stage. I thought we'd get to snoop around her house, which would be in some kind of splendor, either in all-out glamour or cat-lady devastation. But it turned out all the figure skater's stuff was pulled out of her house and spread out in the corporate auction house, which from the outside looked like a big, pueblo-type art gallery. Inside, there were clean, big seashell-white rooms connected by a maze of oddly narrow hallways. The walls of the rooms were lined with various medals and trophies—upon inspection, mostly regional competitions—and nicely framed photographs of the skater with various other skaters. We didn't recognize any faces but that of the Asian-American skater, but all the girls were pretty, pulling hard mid-century smiles, bodies held nervously in tight short dresses. All those strong muscles trying to not look strong but sparkly. There were also a few small oil paintings, mainly landscapes, and a few of cats and dogs. I wondered if they were the work of the skater herself because all of them were labeled "Artist Unknown." But aside from stuff you would see at any garage sale or flea market—kitchenware, furniture, books—there was really nothing else. Worse, for Fei Fei obviously, there were no fabulous clothes. We had assumed that at the very least there would be some great '70s skating dresses. But our vision of early Lycra in shades of tangerine, teal, rose-pink and robin's-egg blue did not materialize, as there were literally no skating dresses at all. Worse still, there were no designer clothes: not even knock-offs tailored at department stores, certainly nothing even resembling Pucci (which is what Jean and I were told to look out for specially, clippings of textiles handed out in preparation). Instead, there were racks and racks of black stuff that were clearly not even that old: turtleneck sweaters, blouses, slacks and long pleated skirts, all timeless in the bad way.

Fei Fei frowned as she scanned the clothes, and as she touch-inspected a few things that looked OK, her frown tilted away from thoughtfulness towards fury.

"This is not very 'fabulous' is it," I said to her.

"I'm sorry, Howie. I thought it would be more fun for you, but no, this is not good. It's just a lot of black stuff. Makes me feel like a sale for stuff she bought to wear to her own funeral. I mean, this is not even good stuff from the '80s."

Determined not to be defeated, Jean tugged Fei Fei towards the table of shoes.

"Hey, how about the shoes? Seems like a lot."

Fei Fei did not remove her frown as she allowed herself to be led towards the shoes; I trailed behind them, like I was their kid at the grocery store.

"All these shoes are black also and besides, they are mostly in horrible shape. Why are they even selling them? And actually, half of these aren't even shoes," Fei Fei said.

She was right: what we thought were chic ankle boots were actually ice skates. Unlike the shoes, though, the skates were in pristine shape, the leather uppers hard as cardboard and polished like fetish rubber, the blades scarily sharp and catching light. I found them rather beautiful and told Fei Fei so.

"Are they? Beautiful? Even if we agree that they are, what am I going to do with a hundred pairs of ice skates?" She looked around vaguely as she continued mumbling to us. Sticking her hand in her giant black suede bag, she pulled out a big ivory-backed hairbrush and began brushing the pad of her thumb with it. It might have looked like a nervous gesture to some people, but she was calculating possibilities.

"You could knock the blades off and sell them as cool boots!" Jean joked. I think she was joking?

Fei Fei slowly turned to her with her mouth in a perfectly straight, closed line. Fortunately for Jean, before Fei Fei could say anything to her, we heard a very loud gay male voice coming towards us.

"Hey, Faye! You're here!"

It was the old queen who made us come up here. But

he wasn't an old queen at all, even though that's what Jean called him; I guess it was affection rather than description. He was probably older than us but not by much: at most, in his early forties, a white guy, slightly balding head with otherwise thick hair cropped to an elegant, purposeful length. He wore a dark blue turtle-neck sweater and because the knit was fine I could see he was in pretty good physical shape. With the dark blue sweater and slightly darker blue pants, he wore expensive-looking black loafers so slick they looked wet. Over one tit was an enormous enamel brooch in an abstract shape and even more abstract colors that just blinded you. I wondered how the brooch stayed on the thin sweater without dragging down and snagging; I think his muscly pec acted as a kind of shelf for it. There were silver and gold chains of varying thickness around his wrist, and a couple of thick rings too. Also, a single pearl dangle signifying from his right earlobe. Looking at his pearl, I wished I could wear a signifying earring too, but I learned as a teenager that being a male ballet dancer, holding girls up, lifting girls up, dropping and catching girls, having something dangling from your earlobe was a liability to all involved; my ears are unpierced, although my left nostril isn't.

The old queen who wasn't old came over to us and Jean said something like, Hey Dude. They hugged tightly and lingeringly. He then gave Fei Fei a tight hug as well; tight but brief. Fei Fei held him in return while barely touching him.

"Good to see you again Faye. You made it! How long has it been now? I think not since you came up to Guerneville with Jean last year."

"It's Fei Fei," she corrected him without emotion, but with a wide smile that showed no teeth. In the end, it was a very sweet smile but the instant it takes to go from neutral to smiling seemed slowed down to minutes, if not hours. Observing Fei Fei complete her smile, Jean just burst out laughing. The not really old queen went very pink about the ears but he smiled gamely back, nice white teeth gleaming.

Fei Fei was wearing a vintage dance leotard made with neither nylon nor polyester but very small gauge wool. The stretch had almost totally gone from it from all the wear, and it made its very pale beige color even paler. She wasn't wearing a brassiere so she should have looked naked, but the way the sleeve hit a few inches above her big knobby wrists made her look not just dressed, but prim. With this she wore a knee-length skirt made of matte leather in what was, miraculously, the same beige as the leotard. As she walked her shoes made a ton of noise: they were very high-heeled clogs in natural varnished wood. They were fixed to her feet with very wide strips of furry black suede that were stapled to the wood with big-headed brass nails. She shouldn't have, but she looked very professional.

"Jean, you're looking well. And who is this?" The guy looked me up and down like I was a potential victim. Weirdly, it made me feel not unsexy.

"This is our friend Howie. Howie, this is Jamie."

"Hi Howie, a pleasure. You are like a Jennifer Beals for the new millennium!"

I too was wearing a dance leotard, and I am a professional dancer, but I most definitely did not look professional. My leotard was a black short-sleeved Capezio leotard. It was a women's leotard, but I like having the deep scoop in the back to let my scapulae breathe when I work. I snipped the seam joining the two halves at the crotch and wore it like a t-shirt. Even though I had bought it only a few months ago and it was made entirely of Lycra stretchy enough to be an industrial-strength rubber band, it was worn down and webby, both from sweat and friction. I had just come home from rehearsal when Fei Fei and Jean picked me up, so I had on my rehearsal clothes—said leotard, jockstrap, and baggy grey sweatpants with the ankle elastics cut off—and my dance-and-get-home layers over it: an oversized white sweatshirt with white silk screen of "SYRACUSE UNIVERSITY" and the university seal, cut across the stomach so the tabs of my leotard hung down and flopped about.

"If we're going to some fancy estate, shouldn't I put on more formal clothes?" I had asked the gals.

"No, you're fine," said Fei Fei. "Also, we're not going to an estate, it's an *estate sale*. Come on, we're running late."

I dumped kibbles in the bowl for Delilah, my dog, and gave her a speedy deep nuzzle. At the words "Bye Delilah" she vibrated, and made her big searchlight eyes, knowing full well I'd be back; the big, beautiful manipulator.

I took Jamie's New Millennium Jennifer Beals comment

as a compliment. The way he was looking at me was predatory and gratifying. With no shame nor coquetry, his eyes lingered at my crotch: I wondered if he could figure out the outline of my cock. On the ride up I was, again, like a child: Fei Fei drove with Jean riding shotgun, me in the back seat pointing out in dumb bitchery the trailerish homes between Richmond and Napa Valley nestled around and beyond the little valleys made of nail salons, Michaels craft stores, Home Depots. While making lame giggles at the multiple signs for the Gun and Doll Show, I pulled my right leg free out of the sweatpants to take off my sweaty jock strap. Once I stepped out of the right strap of my jock strap, I could pull the whole thing off by sliding it over my left leg and the right half of the pants. It sounds all contorting and complicated, but it's easy for me; I've always been more apt at flexibility than strength. And even though I did have to flash commuters and truckers who got too close, it was nevertheless my attempt at modesty, like the trick of taking your brassiere off with your sweater still on.

"Jamie, man, this is not exactly what you said it would be," Jean complained in a voice that was jovial.

"I know, I know. I didn't see the actual lot until this morning. But I'm sure there's something here, right? I mean, there are a lot of skates and trophies."

Fei Fei seemed to speak through a shut mouth: "Yes, but I run a vintage clothing store. You can't wear a trophy."

Having heard the word "crap" through her actually spoken words, Jamie looked back at her, finally matching her coldness: "Well, I'm really sorry about that. Like I said, I had no idea, otherwise I wouldn't have wasted your valuable time." The word "sorry" sounded like a meat cleaver hitting bone.

No one said anything, and I think Jamie quickly decided it wasn't worth it. "Listen, as long as I got you up here, why don't you look around, just for fun? I'll be done in an hour and then I'll treat us all out to dinner. And drinks." He looked right at me with a most charming smile as he said this.

Fei Fei shrugged, but warmly. "You don't have to treat us, but yes, OK, let's all just go get drinks and dinner. I'm sorry if I'm kind of crabby, Jamie. I know it's not your fault." Fei Fei had a kind of high voice, but as she always spoke so softly, carefully and definitively, it felt low and solemn, and also a bit like playing at tippy-toes with her index and middle fingertips.

Eventually we came upon something somewhat desirable: a square oil painting, painted with skill and realism, of a young adolescent white girl with long sandy hair, combed back from broad forehead, flowing down over each shoulder. The painting cut the girl off at about chest level, and the cascading hair, too, was cut off. She wore a white lace collar over a plain very dark green sweater that could have been black, and an expression that could have been a smile. Her eyes were looking up and to the right, focused but daydreaming. The girl took up only the bottom third of the painting under a painting within the painting that showed another girl, an old-fashioned one, in profile, reading a tiny book. The old-fashioned girl was also white and blond, eyes cast down toward her text, hair piled high in weird knots and leaning a rather buxom body against a fat white cushion. The whole thing was about 24 inches on each side and its frame was cheap, non-committal curlicues in porous wood splintering dulled gilt. Frame notwithstanding, we all agreed that we liked the painting. Fei Fei marked it in her catalogue; the starting bid was ridiculously low.

"It doesn't have any artist marks on it. I wonder if the skater herself painted it," said Jean.

"It seems unlikely," said Fei Fei. "None of these paintings look at all alike, stylewise."

"Maybe she faked her style. Maybe she was schizophrenic!" Jean said, and Fei Fei looked at her with a look that said, "You're stupid but also cute."

"You could use it for your store," I said to Fei Fei. "Not to sell, I mean. You could hang it inside, behind the counter and then maybe you could have someone make like a simple line drawing version of it that you could use for a logo."

"That's an idea," Fei Fei said with openness.

Fei Fei's shop was called Christabel. It really sounded like some shop in Koreatown full of cheapo knockoffs with brand names all misspelled ESL-style, but actually, apparently, so said Fei Fei, it is the title of a poem by Samuel Taylor Coleridge, the name of a thousand-year-old lesbian vampire, or a princess who gets seduced by the lesbian vampire.

Suddenly, across the room there was a guy looking in our direction—looking at me. He was dressed like a laborer and I think he was one; there were other guys of varying sizes and ages and ethnicities moving around him and around a big sofa wrapped in the blue quilting of a moving blanket, bound up with brown cellophane tape. You could only see the arched wooden legs, but the blue of the moving quilt was so electrifying, the white threads of its quilting so pretty that it could pass for an artsy sofa, as wrapped up as it was. With me in my big white sweatshirt and the moving guy in his big maroon one, we could have been weird mirror images. But not really: his sweatshirt was fully intact, and he had the hood flipped up just casually so you could see ragged sandy hair jutting out from it. He had a small, narrow head and face, with closely set eyes and freckles upon a big broken Greco-Roman nose and sensuous, full lips that were open as if he were breathing through them. He was wearing a very thick, ornate silver and turquoise bracelet on his left wrist that made his wrist look delicate and his whole self, like a douchebag. I'm not sure that delicateness and douchebagness were inconsequential to one another. I moved around the gals a bit as they chatted and indeed, the guy's eyes followed me. I was instantly filled with desire but nipping at the heels of that desire was an intense feeling of obstruction that made me want to puke.

The moving guy's face reminded me of Daniel, the first man who ever fucked me. They had the same look, features that looked crushed between sallow cheekbones. Daniel had been more than twenty years older than me; I was sixteen when we met. We were in the stall of a public restroom in the park where he was head groundskeeper.

He made me straddle his face while he sat on the toilet and sucked my cock slowly, methodically, using a feeling of self-satisfaction as well as his tongue to make me feel hot. He was jerking himself off while he sucked and, just as I was about to come, he spat me out. He put two of his fingers in his mouth. I let out a small sound of surprise, not pain, as he eased the first finger in and crooked and wiggled it inside me, searching. He found and then began petting my prostate, and I felt something thin and very sharp shoot upward inside me, bouncing off vertebrae and bumping small squishy organs, paving the weird road to my heart and brain. He wedged a second finger in. Like this Daniel petted and thrust in and out of me until sperm sprayed out of my cock, my hands gripping his shoulders. He had a narrow but surprisingly powerful chest, and as I stared at the white-grey sperm clotting his greying chest hair, I could see his pectoral muscles clench and pull into his breastbone. He relaxed, and put his hands around my waist and caressed it, spreading the inside of me on my skin.

"Wow, look. I can almost span my hands around your waist," he said.

I was too young to feel embarrassed by his words, and instead I felt earnestly admired. I stuck my neck out awkwardly to kiss him, but smiling, he averted his face. At sixteen, I had wanted desperately to kiss and be kissed by a man, but Daniel never did kiss me. We made regular these public restroom encounters, but as much as I begged and cajoled him he never stuck his tongue in my mouth, never pressed his lips to mine, and never fucked me with his cock, even though he fucked me in all sorts of different ways with one, two, three fingers, his lips and tongue. A couple times after the first time he told me that he had been with his boyfriend Robert for almost 15 years, and they were renovating their heritage Victorian house. I never did meet Robert.

"I wonder why I like men," I blurted out.

Neither Jean nor Fei Fei looked particularly surprised.

"What do you mean?" Jean asked.

"I mean, in general I don't like men. When I get to know them, I feel like most of them are jerks."

"That's because you are like us," said Fei Fei. "You have a desire that's been disconnected from the phallus."

"Oh Fei Fei," Jean sighed. Jean was a soft butch wearing thick tortoiseshell glasses, with a shock of thick black hair full of cowlicks that was cut in the style of a middle-aged dad, all of which looked quite attractive on her. She was a natty dresser; I've never seen her in t-shirt or jeans, except at the beach once, she wore a loose black shirt with weird dark jam shorts. Today she was wearing a crisp black button-down shirt like pajamas, with dark grey piping on the collar and pocket plackets.

"Because we have moved our desire a good, significant distance away from paternalism," continued Fei Fei, ignoring Jean. "Away from the phallus, including the penis and moved it to…inappropriate aspects of the self, like dress, or attitude, or personality, or vagina."

"Yes, that's right. I feel that way . . . except for the vagina part," I said. "I mean, I know I like penises, I like holding them in my hand, my mouth, my ass, but honestly, I don't even think about cock until I find myself naked in front of another naked man. Most of the time I'm thinking about that other stuff stuck to the guy—like yeah, his personality, or attitude, or even clothes. But his penis . . . it doesn't seem either like destination or lure. It's not like I expect the cock to be great because the guy acts great. I wish I were into women."

"But it's not like it's that way with women, either," Jean said. "It's not like, just because I see a hot girl, I am divining her vagina."

Fei Fei said to me: "What you're asking is: Do you fall in love with a man because of his cock that you've not seen yet? Is love tolerating his repellent personality or despicable politics or ugly face because you know that you hold his cock so well? Or is love your tolerance of his inadequate cock because he has a handsome face, inspiring politics, or fun personality?"

"Here comes Jamie," said Jean. I crooked my neck over my shoulder and saw him walk swiftly, bouncingly towards us, and I knew we'd fuck in the near future.

OoO

BEFORE THIS SPACE IN WHICH WE WERE SITTING BECAME a lobby, all barriers of steel slats and glass sheets as well as black and Latin people wearing deceptively casual uniforms to prevent just anyone from drifting up to the second and third floors of a company for an app that facilitated the delivery of takeout food, before any of us knew that "app" was a contraction of the word "application program," this space was actually a nice restaurant a kitty corner off Market Street near Valencia. We didn't eat here too often, not because of the price—expensive but not exorbitant—but because it was a magnet for the kind of old San Franciscans who donated their old Armani and Chanel to the Catholic charity shops, knew about Tuesday nights out and of course had regular seats to the opera and ballet, and thus could potentially be my patrons, whom I'd want to avoid. That is, if I were good enough to have proper patrons—if I could just stop being such a loser.

This restaurant was one of those restaurants with a lot of odd bravado: there were a billion options for beer but only two shit wines, and the food was underwritten with dainty flavors but they served a ton of it on plates that were chipped and vintage. The kitchen was exposed like a diner so that all the cooking was framed in the oblong rectangle of the art film ratio. Jeb was a sous chef at this restaurant. Like a classical bust, all I could see of Jeb when I saw him there was above tit-level. He had dark blonde hair framing his faded, slightly ratty baseball cap, and his face was handsome, a nose with long equine nostrils under a slightly tilted tip and a sweet generous mouth, the kind that smiled by stretching it wider and pulling its corners down rather than up. From this vantage point I couldn't tell at all about his body, but I felt certain he had a nice body, even though I'd been with plenty of men whose handsome faces led down to unattractive bodies. I was stealing glances at his slightly sneering face, although I think that was just the backward-and-up tilt of his nostrils and stretched-frown-smile, so my certainty about his body was a most superficial one based on my stereotypes about men.

The way I lean so hard on stereotypes about men, sometimes I can't tell if it's all my years living on the border of lesbian separatism or that I'm really the worst of the backwards kind of regressive person who thinks that men and women are fundamentally different inside and the only true happiness is marrying a man who will keep you barefoot and pregnant. Of course I'm a male human being so I can't get pregnant, and I know that lesbian separatism is pretty difficult for a gay male. I can't get pregnant but I prefer being barefoot; the dykes who hang out with me these days could get pregnant but don't like being barefoot; butches have their stomping boots and high femmes, sex kitten heels or stomping boots. Maybe it's the current trend against hippies—except rich Gucci hippies in thousand-dollar faded jeans tacked with exotic feathers. Anyway, it was all a hopeless place from which to fall in love with a man, and I felt like falling in love with Jeb.

Wearing stomping boots of my own, I was having a late, late dinner with two friends who used to be a couple, wearing their stomping boots. Then I saw this guy, Jeb, working in the exposed kitchen, and my friends became absolutely bored that I found him cute. Fei Fei and Val bounced gestures and aphorisms off each other like they were still in love and fucking. Fei Fei was Asian and femme and Val was white and butch but they kind of looked like sisters, especially tonight. Val's short blond hair had grown out a bit to resemble the kind of louche eyeball-stabbing shag of an Italian bisexual gigolo from the 1960s. However, tonight she had greased it all back with a ton of waxy pomade in the style of the wrong boy from the 1950s, which revealed her unusually high hairline; it reminded you of a space alien and a middle-aged man losing his hair, but also made her look very handsome. A week earlier, Fei Fei got her waist-length hair cut into a neat shoulder-length bob that swung cheerfully. Tonight, she had put a ton of styling cream into it and combed it straight back, making her look like she had just climbed out of a swimming pool. With this style, I noticed that she too had a very high hairline, so while they looked terribly different, my two friends also looked terribly related, sitting flush next to each other across from me, making fun of me and my dumb desires. The way Fei Fei and Val were talking to each other about Jeb was a shell game in which they were both confidence women making an intricate dance out of shuffling walnut shells before me, except there were no empty shells: each one cupped the magic ball, except the magic ball was some irresistible trinket—maybe a tiny brass cupid with cunning details of curls and arrow, lovingly polished; a day-glo green feather shockingly sharp to the touch; a bean-shaped button off a couture jacket; a doll's stiletto shoe; a chipped tip of a dog's tooth. And they let me keep the trinket after I pointed insecurely at the shell that protected it.

Actually, all three of us looked somewhat alike. We were all thin—I'm sure our combined weight barely cracked 300 pounds—and we all had high foreheads. Except mine was due to the inevitably receding hairline of a biological male approaching 30. My hair was the opposite of Fei Fei's: since I was between ballet seasons, I was letting the floppy part of my hair grow out into a chin-length shaggy bob—although I would probably have to cut it just as it became a proper bob because even though my hair grows fast, it's not as fast as the Winter Season creeping up on a dancer.

Most male ballet dancers, I think, have a chronic and pathological fear of looking too feminine—fey, girly, femme, faggotty—even if they are actually homosexual. I've never had that fear. To our dinner I almost wore something that Fei Fei gave me from her shop, a stretchy, clingy velvet mock turtleneck tee in a disturbing eggplant shade. Instead, I was wearing an old Cramps tour t-shirt from 1990 with an image of a Bettie Page-type diva in a bikini firing off a machine gun. The shirt was an original but I didn't buy it in 1990, when I was just an out-of-it teenager. Also, I couldn't sing you a single song by the Cramps but they sure made some beautiful concert souvenirs. Making the dripping horror movie typeface of their band name in soft pink outlined in bile green showed especially good taste.

I had tucked a knot in the shirt in a way so that it looked like I had a hugely deformed but very artistic-looking "outsie" belly button. You couldn't see my real "innie" belly button though because I also had on these old black jeans, worn down to ladders of black thread under the crotch and on the thighs. They were women's jeans from the 1980s: a style of Wranglers funnily named "Bare Back"—because they had no back pockets. I didn't realize that in the 1980s women didn't want or need back pockets; surely they didn't believe back pockets made their butts look big? The ones I was wearing had a button fly that was uncovered, so that you could see the four silver buttons leading up to the one that closed over my navel. I could button it up but there was no way I was going to be able to eat cheese or pasta—not that I ever should, anyway. It wasn't uncomfortable, although I can't say I enjoyed the sensation: I could feel my left leg going to sleep. On the inside of the waistband someone had written in black Sharpie: "RN." The letters became visible only after the first year of washings, as the black dye of the denim faded away from the more indelible blackness of the pen. Since they came to me five years ago unworn stiff with the tags still stapled to the back pocket, I wasn't sure why RN felt the need to mark the jeans. I hoped she hadn't died or something before she got a chance to wear them.

"These pants are kind of killing me," I complained. "They're slicing me in half."

Fei Fei said, "Jeans were invented for manual laborers to move about freely and stick a lot of tools in their pockets and now you—sorry, we—wear them akin to corsets. Chain stitching cutting like steel or whale bone boning."

Val said, "Corset or self-castrating machine."

I nodded. "Sometimes I wish I really were transsexual. Bottom surgery would be worth it so I could properly wear some tight jeans."

My friends laughed but they also knew that I wasn't 100 percent joking, either. I turned to look at the handsome sous chef.

"Oh, but he looks just like Chris Isaak in *Silence of the Lambs*," I sighed.

"Chris Isaak was in *Silence of the Lambs?*" Fei Fei asked.

"Briefly," Val answered.

And I followed: "He was a sweaty FBI or SWAT officer. I'm also sick of feeling like just because I'm gay I have to fall in love with gay guys. Sometimes when I'm out with people—not you guys, but like, work people or straight people—I point out a cute guy, and they're like, 'Oh, how do you know he's gay?' I mean, who cares. We don't need permission to find a person attractive or loveable. Is it because I'm gay that people think my saying 'I'd like to fuck this guy' means 'I'm going to fuck this guy'?"

"Basically, yeah," Val said. "If someone says to you, 'I desire you,' that doesn't mean they are going to do anything about it, it's not like a marriage proposal or a rape. You can react. Because you are a person, you have an infinite number of ways to react to expressions of desire. But people are afraid to be told that they are desired."

"People are always available to fall in love with," I said. "My feelings don't exist just to be reciprocated. Can't I just have my feelings, put them out in the world, whether they are reciprocated or not? They are just feelings. I feel like I am totally available to everyone to desire, so I just assume everyone else is the same. But when I think that I'm available to everyone . . . sometimes I can't tell whether I'm being slutty or generous."

"But why do you need to put those two feelings in conflict with one another?" asked Fei Fei "They are false dichotomies, because as you must know, that's just the same feeling. But 'slutty' makes it seem like you are doing something wrong, whereas 'generous' makes it seem like you are overvaluing your sexuality."

Val frowned and smiled at the same time. "I think I understand what Howie's saying," she said. "You're parsing a little too much with his words. Isn't the whole issue that, as usual, it's all unfair? Unfair that we gay people have to bear the brunt of straight people, well, straight *men*, who are allowed to find anyone and everyone desirable, and they have pushed this presumptive permission to extremes and turned feeling into actual rape. They've erased the difference between words—loving words—and bad acts. And then we as gay people have to pay the price for it. Like if we fall in love with, or try to fall in love with, people who are not gay, we're doing something inappropriate or violating."

"Yes, you're right."

"Because in fact, women don't really rape. It's straight men who have truly raped the world and then the rest of us have to deal with it. Because of them, any sexual scene that we play from our structurally and institutionally disempowered place that might play with consent or be at all ambiguous has to be potentially 'rape.'"

We all nodded and took a gulp of our drinks.

I announced, "OK I have to go pee out all this wine. It's a miracle that these fucked up jeans have been pressing into my kidneys for this long already and I've been able to hold it."

I got up from my chair and took a couple steps and tipped over. If I wasn't born with a nose that already looked broken, a destiny of inviting bars with particularly hard and slippery floors certainly would have made certain it turn out that way. I wasn't drunk and the floor wasn't liquidy marble nor freshly waxed, but I tipped over anyway. I would have fallen on my face and maybe broken my broken-looking nose but for Jeb, who appeared out of nowhere and caught me.

"Whoa, your boots," he said.

My boots had eight-inch shafts, laced through eyelets on the bottom half and hooks on the top. Instead of lacing them tight all the way to the top, I just laced the eyelets and then wrapped the remaining lace around the ankle. The hooks of the right boot had snagged the laces, binding my ankles and hobbling me.

I tried to get up on my own but couldn't; my legs had locked up. Gently, he tipped me back up as if I were an old toy on a shelf. I saw that his face captured that specific moment in a young guy's life—usually in the second or third year of college, although Jeb was obviously older than that—when the bloom of youth is just about to go off. The bloom is high and rich, dangling off the nodes of big bones, like he could become anything with the whim of the wind: patriarch, sweet boyfriend, babydaddy, dumb husband, faggot, yuppie, woman. Cheeks flush fast, tender coral lips reveal teeth often, and eyes have that cut-glass brightness that looks very close to stupidity.

"Oh, fuck. Thanks so much," I said, balancing on my hog-tied tips.

"You're welcome."

"I'm not drunk."

"I know," he said. "Do you want to get drunk though? I'm off in about twenty minutes."

I could feel that through the chef scrubs, he had a nice body after all. He smelled like cooked meat and vanilla. Val and Fei Fei were smiling together: *chipped tip of a dog's tooth.*

Forty minutes later Jeb and I got to my place, where my dear Delilah was waiting for me. I had been waiting for Jeb, by instruction, at the service entrance of the restaurant, which was perhaps the most un-service-like service entrance ever, as its colorful, gilded '80s-camp-roccoco door faced, of all streets, Haight Street. Eventually, Jeb walked out amidst the steam of dishes cleansing, walking a beat-up bicycle in indigo, with a kind of shimmer.

"Do you want a ride?" he asked.

I answered yes and he maneuvered me against his butt and me holding onto him, wobbling off we went the few blocks to Delilah, already pointed towards us, stomach to the floor, front paws forward framing her face, hind legs tucked out behind her at an angle so that she could cross her ankles off her left side. Her tail is so big that when she rests it dovetails against her haunch and the crook of her hind legs, it looks like a small animal of its own, bristly-soft black, white, and rust. Delilah is 75 pounds and when she stands up she is almost as tall as I; when she walks alongside me she looks bigger than me. She was laying right before the door of my apartment as I knew she would be when she smells or hears or otherwise senses me coming home: the tip of her nose leaves just enough space for me to open the door. As soon as I opened the door I heard her happy noise mixed with the small warning growl that vibrated her black lips in readiness for a loud, protective bark, possibly bared teeth.

I made eye contact with her and put my loosened palm toward her, arm straight, the pose of the Supremes, "Stop! In the Name of Love."

"It's OK, lady," I said in my stern-soft voice.

Delilah looked over at Jeb. Her eyes were the color of milk chocolate if milk chocolate could become translucent and hard as caramel, set in a face the color of wheat described in English novels, rimmed in black flesh. Weirdly, there was a thin line of black fur that went past the black flesh of her eye opening and formed a pleasing, oblong tip nearly to the bridge of her nose, like eyeliner drawn past and around the natural opening of your eye so your eyes look not only bigger, but more mystical, ancient, and futuristic: Mod.

"Aww, is her name Lady?" Jeb's voice had become bleary. He closed the door behind him and pressed up right against me with his hips and stomach, no hands.

"No, her name is Delilah."

"Hi Delilah. You're a nice-looking girl." Jeb let his hand hover gently above her long snout, apparently knowing to let her sniff his fingers first, although by this time, Delilah had intuited—even before I did, or would, eventually—that Jeb was not a threat, though not necessarily not dangerous. Delilah and I were both always discovering together what makes a guy a bastard. She raised herself a little, smelled, and sunk down to her original position, still suspicious.

"I have to take a piss really bad," Jeb said.

I gave him a little push.

"Well, the bathroom's right through there, dummy."

"You seem like you'd always insult the guys you go out with."

I wanted to ask, "Are we going out?" and it is a wonder given how drunk I was that I didn't actually say it. Instead I said, "I'm going to get into something more comfortable. Do you want a scotch? Or beer?"

"Scotch would be great." He stretched his mouth into that frown-smile and staggered a little into the bathroom, closing the door behind him.

I unlaced my boots and took them off. I held them up and gave their toes a kiss of gratitude. Then I went into the kitchen, poured Black and White into two cups and put them next to my bed. My bed was just a mattress and box spring on the floor, but I have expensive sober bedding and the shiny nylon quilting of the box spring, with its pattern of black line-drawn orange, pink and yellow flowers all over a bright green background, was kitschy enough to have some pride in. I used to have a proper bed frame, but since Delilah's hip dysplasia began surfacing, I got rid of the frame so she could get on my—our—bed without pain. I hope I don't have to get rid of the box spring anytime too soon, not because then my apartment might really look indigent, but because that would mean Delilah's hips are truly bad.

In truth, because my apartment was so small and strangely shaped, it made better sense not to have too much furniture. I lived on the first floor of a very narrow Victorian in Hayes Valley, one of those little streets that are really glorified alleyways bearing names of flowers. An address that looks cute on envelopes, except all I ever got was junk mail and bills. Like most Victorians in San Francisco, the first floor really felt like the second floor because of the rather steep walk-up, although this one was not as steep as most, and no one lived under me. When you came up and through the front door, you saw a long straight flight of stairs to the left and the door to my apartment to the right, another door down the end of the hall in between, and that was it. That last door led out into a little stony backyard that nobody, including Delilah, ever used. My apartment had clearly been a sitting room that was converted into a studio apartment; you knew its walls were just longing to be reunited with its original and proper hallway. You walked through my door, around my bed, a small Aiwa stereo system sitting on the floor under a small dining table with a couple blond-wood chairs with black velvet seats, little knick-knacks and paperback books on the baseboard platform of the baseboard heating all along the rim of the walls, then you moved into a tiny kitchen. The kitchen had the most space out of any of the rooms in my place. A luxe kitchen is where you can watch the world outside as you wash dishes, but my kitchen was not luxe; it had a window, but not above the sink. So I did my squats there during the off-season, which was why across from the range there was a barbell along with a stack of weights. And then a tiny bathroom beyond that. The shape of the apartment was not a rectangle but also not quite a horseshoe; it was just kind of an architectural bulge, walls and floor that justified the tall beautiful windows. There was barely any wall space for shelves or art, which was fine because I didn't really have art or the need for shelves (I had baseboards). There were only two real wall spaces, one next to the front door against which was a huge old-fashioned wardrobe that held all my clothes and shoes, and the other over the head of my bed, where I had a framed autographed photo of the great ballet dancer Julio Bocca.

I took off all my clothes and lay on the bed. At first I lay on my back with my legs spread, not as a come-on but because I was tired and it felt good to stretch out, pointing my toes, flexing my arches. Then I thought maybe I should think about a come-on, so I turned over on my stomach, raising and resting myself on both elbows, legs spread, but not too much. Then it struck me that this pose might be too precious, too gay, too eager, too evocative of a winking anus, but before I had a chance to move into a more chill pose, Jeb was standing at the foot of the bed. He had taken off his jacket but still had his shirt on, but nothing else. The flesh of his legs looked pale and cold. His legs and pubic bush were very hairy—thick and blond, blonder than the hair on his head. I could see that he had a huge tattoo on the front of each leg, curling from mid-thigh to mid-calf. It looked like some kind of fish, two of exactly the same design. Absurdly I thought: salted mackerel. I could see the tattoos clearly because the hair on his leg was so light it formed a gauzy pane over his skin. He wasn't hard but it was sexier to me that he wasn't; his limp, prettily-shaped dick thick and hanging between slightly bowed legs.

He looked as though he was about to say something, but nothing came out of his mouth. I turned and sat up, pulling my knees up and tucking my feet under me, ankles crossed. He fell onto his knees, onto the bed right up against me. I reached over and held the collar of his shirt. It was a heavy kind of canvas work shirt.

"Do you want to take this off?" I asked.

"No," he replied with certainty but also carelessness.

"Let me rephrase myself. Take this off."

He took the shirt off, pulling it over his head as if it were a t-shirt. He struggled a bit, and I could hear the ping and tap of a button popping off into a corner.

I looked up and my field of vision was filled with his neck, a square of clear skin, raised pores dotting it, stretched over a bulls-eye of hard round bone, almost a hexagon, his Adam's apple. He had a large brown spot that covered half of his Adam's apple, but as I focused I saw that it wasn't a perfect circle but had a bite taken out of it where it rested on bone in a kind of crescent—a waning moon, waxing? I could never remember the difference. I thought that I would love a painting of this clean neck, unexpectedly powerful and innocent as a classic column, cut down to a small square the size of a handkerchief. I'd hang it between window frames.

I reached around and touched his butt cheeks. He flinched a little but didn't move, so I caressed them slowly. The skin of his butt was kind of dry, and I could feel a couple little pimples. It was, surprisingly, totally hairless, although I wouldn't call it smooth.

Delilah watched us from the foot of the bed, curving her big body into a crescent wedged between the edge of the bed and the part of the baseboard upon which balanced a little stoneware calf. Her eyes doppled onto mine then they moved slowly but alertly to Jeb. I knew she did this not out of any genuine curiosity but habit and training. When I first got Delilah, she would climb up on the bed when I had sex. My sounds when fucking seemed to telegraph to her that the guys in bed with me were trying to hurt me. The guys I fucked during those first few weeks with Delilah didn't stick. Sometimes the guy tried to be cute and seduce Delilah as well, but that never worked. If the guy was the irritable type, he would get dressed and leave. If he were patient, I would push pause, get out of bed and drag the girl by her scuff and lock her in the bathroom. But then she just emitted a high, puppyish whine of distress from behind the door, so even the patient guys didn't call again. It took a while but eventually I trained her to distinguish between sounds of pleasure and sounds of distress, and from there, Delilah learned to distinguish between guys and lovers. She still took fairly high level Fear Anger Stress poses when a strange guy entered our home, but as soon as he took off his clothes, she relaxed and let the humans be. But she still liked to tuck herself in her special corner and keep an eye out—just in case.

I could see that Jeb still wasn't hard, although there was clear glutinous stuff dripping from the tip of his penis. Keeping one hand on his butt, I reached over with my other hand and moved him round to the head of the bed. He was obedient when I leaned him against the wall. Then I put myself in a super awkward position in between his sprawled legs. I was on my stomach again but resting up on my forearms with my palms down like paws, my entire lower body balancing on the points of my knees, bum tilting up, toes bent back. I smelled fresh urine and saw cute driblets on his piss slit. I was getting ready to suck his cock when he put both hands on my shoulders.

"I don't want you to do that," he said. "But stay that way. You look sweet."

While I stayed like a statuette, he spat, through closed teeth, one thick slow stream of saliva onto his cock and worked it with his palms until he was properly hard. Then he got up, stepped gingerly around me and fucked me from behind. He didn't penetrate me with any wiggle of care or decorum; he just pushed the tip of his penis into my anus. He let out the smallest of grunts as his foreskin struck the skin of my butthole. While he pushed and pulled himself into me, he buried his face into my hair and grabbed my tits. He squeezed my erect nipples between his knuckles while caressing my chest with his fingertips. He must have been used to small women because his caress was easy and warm, like he was comfortable with a body like mine. He fucked me hard and fast, and within a few minutes he was done, coming inside me.

For a long time after he kept his penis inside me and rested heavily against my body. But his drunk lethargy had electricity to it. I could feel that his cock was still hard in me, and if not hard, at least swollen. When he finally pulled out, I could feel a lot of his semen rushing out of me and streaming down from my still-stretched butthole and onto the inner edges of my thighs. After he pulled out, he shifted a bit on his knees. He grinned dazzlingly at me and then dove down and began to eat me out. He rimmed eagerly and sloppily, but with a palpable singularity of drive. He slurped up his own spunk in between passionately kissing my butthole, now exhaling into its normal small budded ring. Jeb's tongue was pointed and curling, saliva flowing copiously. Finally, he kissed me with that mouth.

"Are you a good cook?" I asked, my mouth gummed with his spunk and my own ass.

"Yeah. I'm a pretty good cook," he answered, and stuck his tongue back into my mouth. We lay next to each other, my back into his chest. Delilah woke up at the silence of our non-movement, and then dropped back to sleep. Soft infant barks.

I asked, "Are you some kind of Scandinavian?"

He didn't answer except to kiss me really sweetly. Then he pulled away just far enough to reply: "Finnish, mostly. You are Korean."

"How did you know that?"

"I have experience."

"Experience with what? Asians?"

"Yeah, I guess. I like them."

"Do you like Asian girls more than black girls? Or white girls?"

"You ask a lot of questions."

"I like to learn things."

"OK. What else do you want to learn?"

He started to kiss me again and began jerking me off. I realized that I hadn't come yet, although I was very hard and my whole body felt fuzzy with desire.

“What do you think about abortion?” I asked.

“I’m for it,” he replied.

“Are you joking?”

“No. Are you?”

“No; I never joke about abortion. I’m glad you believe in a woman’s right to her own body.” He was rubbing the shaft of my cock in a way that made it feel fragile, an exotic violent animal being taunted through cage bars. I reached over and held his cock, which had become rock hard again; we were about the same size.

“I guess I do like Asian girls more than any other ethnicity,” he said. “And obviously, some guys.”

I thought he would fuck me with his cock again but instead he gripped with the tips of a few fingers the tip of my penis and started pulling the flesh up in a languid, rhythmic manner—pinching it, pulling up gently, then letting it go, pinching, pulling up, letting go. I felt myself becoming even harder.

“I feel like I should be offended. Should I be offended?” I asked.

“No, you shouldn’t be offended at all,” he answered, pinching, pulling up, and letting go.

0o0

KALA YOUNG KENNEY WAS MY IDOL, BUT I NEVER CALL her that because when I first met her, moments before I got ready to form the word with my mouth, she indicated to me that she thought the word dumb and insulting to us both. So I never said it, but she is it. When she was eighteen, Kala was discovered by a famous director to play a sensitive, poetic high school junior on an idiosyncratic nighttime soap opera. Kala is only four years older than I, but on television she struck me as so much older, which was a fucked-up kind of reality, because playing the role of someone her own age, she gave off the impression that she was an actress in her thirties inadequately playing a teenager. She looked and talked nothing like any teenaged girl I knew. Her eye openings were very narrow, two perfectly measured lines cut with scalpel and squeezed gently open to let out transparent green eyes that seemed to look at everything askance. Her skin was so powdery and white that when they filmed her outside in natural light, she was furry, like a polar bear. When I see Kala in person now, my own skin rings with the memory of my teenage years, which, like Kala's character on her show, were spent in a place with unbearably hard winters and springs that were only Spring in name and calendrical ritual. When I look at her face or hear her voice—this particular day, sending back a vegetarian dish in which she smelled beef broth—I see myself huddling against a world like winter, so unhappy yet filled with baggy optimism for the future, dazzled by the sparkling winter sunlight as I watched clouds of my white breath mix with the pale blue of Marlboro puffs. Almost 15 years later, Kala didn't look so powdery; her whiteness had taken on the toughness of expensive cardstock. But she still talks the same, with that same voice, like sandpaper that looks from a distance like shaved mink.

As I watched Kala sign the bill for our lunch, it was hard for me not to be a little starstruck still. I didn't sense that she was recognized by anyone in the restaurant, occupied, early Wednesday afternoon, by old white women with stiff hairdos, stiffer facial skin and loose necks who probably never saw Kala's show nor the few indie films she did after it ended. But some of the women definitely took a sideways glance at our table and at Kala in particular, and in that environment, like that of redneck small towns, hostile suspicion may as well have been recognition and awe.

We were all downtown, at Saks Fifth Avenue—the main flagship store, not the men's store a few blocks east. Kala was in town from Los Angeles for a week, and she invited Jean, Fei Fei and I to come have lunch and then browse expensive clothes at the trunk show for an

American designer who was known for his couture-constructed clothes that were considered, Kala told us, "intellectual and nonconformist." I figured that the only person Kala cared to have along was Jean, whom she had briefly dated and thus knew what a good "husband" she could be while a girl bought clothes. I knew this myself having witnessed Jean in action with other femmes: she was like a timed IV drip of constructive and flattering comments. Jean could sense exactly when to sit outside the dressing room with the tasteful balance of interest and boredom, which gave off a gratifying masculinity. It was through Jean that Kala knew both Fei Fei and me. By now, Kala and I were good enough friends for sure, but she knew that I'm not the kind of fag who fawns over women's clothes and lays on thick compliments. As for Fei Fei, there always seemed to be a tiny static of tension between her and Kala. Or more likely, the two didn't like each other but it was beneath both their egos to live out the feeling. I was surprised that Fei Fei even accepted the invitation. All through the lunch she seemed barely to eat, and yet eventually her plate was empty and her wine glass kept being refilled. When the bill came, Jean and I put up purely gestural protests to pitch in, but Fei Fei took out her business Amex. The way that Kala picked the credit card up with just thumb and index finger and plopped it back in front of Fei Fei turned the existent tension into a dead mutant rodent but they both smiled with so much loveliness through it all because how dumb, predictable, and stereotypical would that be for two high-dom-femmes to resent each other, to have a notion in their heads, post-1990s, that there couldn't be two or more monarchs in the dyke hive?

The trunk show itself was simultaneously disappointing and beautiful. I had imagined we'd be transported glamorously back in time: models in clothes wandering about in slow motion, soft sharp commentary filling the space in between them, flutes of champagne held to lips while an eagle-faced postmenopausal saleswoman described each garment's details in an intimate but commanding whisper. Actually, there were flutes of champagne, but the clothes hung heavy like slaughtered animals on black velvet-flocked hangers on wheeled, slightly rickety chrome racks. The saleswoman was a bouncy, cheerful young woman in a turtleneck dress made of black wool shot through with little gold fuzz. She smiled toothsomely through what must have been a terrible itch. A slightly less gleaming female assistant moved around filling half-empty champagne flutes as the head saleswoman moved purposely from one upright posed station to another, gushing about the clothes and guiding the designer to various clients. The designer himself hung back a bit from everything, wearing an open-necked black oxford shirt with black pants and surprisingly scuffed boots. His complexion was tough, and with his dark goatee and long dark hair pulled back from his high forehead, he looked like an unlikely combination of professional wrestler, bounty hunter, sculptor, philosophy professor, and older gay man. I'm sure the last was my only factual observation about him. He had a surprisingly soft and gentle voice, and he and

Kala kissed each other's cheeks continentally as Jean, Fei Fei and I grazed the clothes and drank our champagne like interlopers. The clothes were indeed beautiful, especially up close. I had no idea touching fabric could be so wonderful. I touched a voluminous strapless dress that looked like a giant cone with the tip snipped off. It felt as sweet as ice cream and slick as vomit.

"Wow, is this silk? Or satin?" I asked, to no one in particular.

The itchy gleaming saleswoman was suddenly by my side, upright in attention as a guard in a Beefeater cap. "It's duchesse silk. Isn't it lovely?" I nodded dumbly and was about to say it was slick as vomit but Kala pinched it slightly and smiled at the saleswoman. The saleswoman pulled the dress off the rack and gave it to the assistant who already had an armload.

Kala pulled from the rack a taupe dress that looked like a plain long-sleeved white t-shirt with a black knee-length skirt, except that it was really one dress, and the skirt dripped with three rectangles of slightly darker beaded embroidery. She shook the dress in Fei Fei's direction in a way that was playful and aggressive.

"Do you guys want to try anything on? Fei Fei, I think this would look divine on you."

"Yes, why not? You have great taste, Kala," Fei Fei replied sincerely but not without aggression of her own.

I like shopping for clothes, and I don't mind going shopping for clothes with women. But it's a drag to go shopping for clothes with women who don't have their own strong taste. There are a lot of women who go shopping with you because they are not just shopping but "shopping with a gay man." Then, everything they pick out is held up to you as a life-or-death decision and they really just want you to be there to either say they look fabulous or fat. That's why I like going shopping with women who already know what they like, and it happens that most of those kinds of women are lesbians.

Inside the changing room, which was surprisingly huge, Jean and I sat together on the dove-grey upholstered bench and kept chugging our champs while Fei Fei and Kala tried on the clothes. I learned that it was a good thing that both Fei Fei and Kala were so thin because there were only one sample of each style of dress at a trunk show; if you were a client, you're supposed to already have an intimate knowledge of the designer's work, so that you just judge the individual pieces by their outward beauty and put in an order for your size, which then is fitted more precisely on you once it has been actually made.

Fei Fei took off her clothes, revealing panties and no bra, and downed her two-thirds full glass in one gulp. Kala gave her body a skeptical gaze but her words were lilted, warm, even.

"Fei Fei, you know it's not great to drink so much before trying on clothes. You get bloated, and you don't get a nice feeling for the clothes. You noticed I didn't drink at all at lunch."

"Yes, I know you get bloated if you drink a lot and yes, I noticed you didn't drink at all. But personally I'd rather be as bloated as possible while trying on clothes so I know I can wear them even if I gain a little weight, rather than feeling good in the dressing room then being saddled with a dress that will always be a little too tight."

Kala looked at Fei Fei for a few seconds, like she was going to say something, but in the end, shrugged and finished taking off her own clothes. She, too, was braless but she was also not wearing panties; instead, she had a perfect Hitler mustache between her legs. As I said, she wasn't as furry as she used to be but I was a little shocked at how freckly she was: dots a couple shades darker than her skin everywhere on her like a cartoon deer. She stepped into the big cone-dress. She literally stepped into it, toes pointed. The dress waited for her, its one big dopey eye unblinking, spread out like an unpitched tent or an uninflated hot air balloon, there on the immaculate plush carpeted floor. Once standing in the middle of the dress, she pulled it up by what appeared to be the lining.

"Howie, can you come help me? Hold up the dress while I zip myself in?"

Fei Fei put one hand on her hip and with the other, took my half-full champagne flute and sipped it. She was getting pink about the cheeks. Fei Fei had put her dress on by this time, and she looked spectacular; better than Kala, even though Kala's dress was a more beautiful object. I went and held up the big fat folds of Kala's dress and saw that the whole dress was attached, by tiny strong stitches, to thin plastic strips that formed the bones of a little grey corset. Kala zipped up the corset and then directed me to help her zip up the outer, conical part of the dress until the whole thing assembled itself with the embrace of her upper torso. Even so, it was slightly too big and kept slipping down, the pink nipples of her tiny breasts popping out.

"Wouldn't this be a great maternity dress? Just for a giggle," Kala said. "Except that you have these teensy plastic bones pressing you into a small shape so maybe not; the outer shell is deceptive. Maybe it would be a good first trimester abortion dress," She spoke in a rhythm that made each word a pushpin with which she was creating a very long map of her thoughts.

She turned onto an unexpected path: "My abortion was too close to ten weeks. They had to put these things that are actually a lot like corset stays, but made of dried seaweed, in my cervix. The doctor put them in the night before, because they needed time to soak up fluid from me and literally stretched me out so they could get in there and evacuate my uterus. The little seaweed stays, I could feel them prickling and then filling up more space, or I thought I felt them prickling and filling up more space. I imagined them as microscopic animals pushing the walls of my cervix to get free.

"Jean, I think we met around then, right? I was so lazy, sleeping eleven hours a day, my dogs around me all the time. Remember Maisie-Pie and Bumbelino and Maggie? Oh those darlings, I miss them. I guess technically Bumby was a cat but I'll always think of him as one of the dogs.

"I had just turned 20, the show had just got canceled, and I was torn between wanting to just sleep and walk my dogs, or get breast implants and really go after big movies, really commit to playing sweet girlfriends or black lipstick alien villains. Well, you guys know, I obviously chose to sleep and walk the dogs. I'd get my agent to schedule auditions and then just not go. I think it was kind of the same with getting pregnant. Or, maybe, subconsciously, I wanted to have a child to go along with the dogs. Why else did I totally miss missing my period? I knew I missed it, and I let the weeks go by, because I wasn't thinking in weeks like a human being with a uterus should. I was living in hours, like a dog, just stockpiling moments of time until sleeping, until walking the dogs, until pissing and shitting, until eating, until puking, until cuddling the dogs, until sleeping. But one day, I was cuddling with Maisie and suddenly I felt my uterus. Maisie-Pie's warm, furry back was brushing against my stomach and it shocked me, like sticking your finger in a socket, or setting off your own car alarm. I thought: there is a fetus inside me, and then: panic. I was like: what is inside me and what am I doing with it? Is it mine when I didn't desire it before he put his sperm inside me? It felt like there was something very foreign lodged in me, and there was: the genetic material of someone else. I knew from science that half of it was me, but it didn't feel like mine. I was overcome with panic like I've never known. Panic to be myself, solely and only myself, again."

Fei Fei sat down on the fluffy floor and picked at the long dragging hem of Kala's dress. "I was much younger than you when I had my abortion," she said, not looking up. "I was sixteen. I thought I was much older because I wasn't a Christian Virgin Girl; I listened to Liz Phair and wore leather chokers and Doc Marters and knew about safe sex and condoms, so I thought I wasn't sixteen but I was still just sixteen. With David, the boy who got me pregnant, my boyfriend, we talked to death about it before it happened. But when the time came to lose our virginities, the agreed-upon time, he didn't put the rubber on. And with all my leather and boots I let him. And while he was inside me, it felt to me like he had left his body, like everything that he was, everything I liked about him, seemed to disappear into his hard dick. The fucking didn't feel bad, but it didn't feel great. What he was doing to me didn't make me forget myself and all I kept thinking was C-O-N-D-O-M but I couldn't stop him, like it was bad manners to stop his thrusting and make him put a condom on. Everything seemed like a bunch of nonsense-colored plastic balls bounding around in a big glass bowl.

"I too had that panic feeling, but right away. I started counting time the day after, and literally the day I figured I missed my period I called Planned Parenthood, used my fake ID for something more productive and life-affirming than beer and cigarettes, and I got the abortion. They didn't put seaweed in me, they just vacuumed up my uterus, and I took the bus home."

"Did you tell David?" I asked. I also wanted to ask Kala about the guy who got her pregnant. I didn't know her then, but as I said, she had been my idol since we were both teenagers and I knew from reading a bitchy profile of her in a fashion magazine (Kala came off as a bitchy; the tone of the journalist was rather friendly) that she was dating a semi-famous baseball player at the time. He wasn't so much famous for being a baseball player as he was for being dumbly handsome. I wanted to ask Kala about the baseball player, but I didn't. Instead, I entered my own memories and ran through a wild field of all the condoms, spread, coaxed, stretched over hard cocks as guys entered me, and the rarer times they did without. Like when Jeb came inside me our first night together. We were so drunk but he knew enough the next morning to apologize profusely and assure me he was HIV negative. I believed him but I was also afraid. The fear went away as we saw each other more and more. I'd be lying sideways, ribs balanced on the bed as Jeb pressed his naked stomach into the small of my back to fuck me steadily. When he got close he would warn me verbally, but not in the urgent grunt of pornography but in a strange calm soft whisper, before pulling out of me and flopping on his back, legs spread, skin gone hot, flushed. His nipples would be hard and standing straight up, straining like antennae. If he had worn one, he snapped the condom off his cock and dropped it on his stomach so he could jerk off until he came in his own pubic hair, his right hand pumping, the back of his left hand pressed into his closed eyes as if he couldn't bear to see the world around him. Watching Jeb splayed out, breathing heavily, forearm still covering his eyes, the forearm that has a deep purple scar from one of many inexorable kitchen accidents, hiding himself, maybe from me, from my big scary feelings with their unretractable claws. The pale peach condom lay curled and dead on his belly, looking like a bizarre small animal, bobbing up and down with its own miniature pulse. Jeb's neck was stretched and vulnerable, and all around us, small sounds of desperation. When I used to let my ex-boyfriend Scott ejaculate inside me the same desperate sounds surrounded us. When Scott's sperm shot onto my helplessly viscous red and purple internal organs instead of into the powdery bubble-tip of the rubber I felt my desperate love for Scott butt up against the sadness and fear of my cells that had nothing great to cling to. And I had realized yet again that the sperm of the guy I loved could not make anything with my internal organs except, possibly, disease.

"No, I didn't tell David," Fei Fei answered my question. "I didn't think it was any of his business, and I didn't need to have any drama. I didn't dump him but I did start to build a wall between me and men in general. There was something about what they could do to me—they could plant this foreign object inside you that you're supposed to love and treasure—that truly shocked me and put me off. I didn't connect that with being a lesbian, and I slept with men on and off until my senior year of college. But having the abortion reminded me there was something deep inside me already that could help me reach who I truly was. An abortion is an artificial menstruation, because menstruation is your body's way of reminding you not to betray yourself. Being poor or dumb or living in Mississippi shouldn't deprive you of the opportunity to be a woman liberated from your uterus and ovaries."

Then Kala's dress slid down again, and everyone in the room laughed along with Kala's silly-face tits, including Kala herself. "Alright," she said. "I need a cigarette. Let's get out of here and get a drink."

As we filed out of the dressing room, I told everyone that I couldn't hang with them; I had a date with a guy that I met online; we planned to meet at the Starbucks on the corner of Bush and Powell, and it was already almost 3 p.m.

"Well, if he's a bust, come find us at El Rio. We had such a late lunch I think we can afford some healthy afternoon boozing," Kala said, then motioned at us to wait while she went to find the designer and the saleswoman. That's when Aaron came up to me.

"Howie?" he said, without touching me but presenting himself to me by simply stepping directly in front of me.

"Yes?" He looked really familiar to me but I couldn't recall his face; I had just seen his photo on my computer seven hours earlier.

"It's me. Aaron?"

"Oh my god. Aaron. Yes. What are you doing here?" At this point, Fei Fei and Jean wandered purposely over to where Kala was conversing with the designer and the saleswoman.

"I have a birthday present to buy for an important female friend, so thought I'd come look around here before we meet, but I looked up and thought I saw you, and it is you." Aaron said. He was holding a tiny silver-paper shopping bag.

"It is me. But you have really good vision."

"Well yeah I do, long distance. But also this store is built like a true panopticon. Like a prison designed deceptively open so that it feels wall-less but in fact everyone can surveil everyone else."

"I know. I mean, you're right about this building and also I know what a panopticon is. Who knew that Saks is a Foucauldian construct, right?"

"Oh wow, you know Foucault. That's really good. It's actually not Foucault but a philosopher named Jeremy Bentham, but I'm still impressed."

"Well, I'm glad you're impressed. I'm not a complete doughnut-hole you know." My voice put its fists on its hips.

He blushed a little. "I'm sorry if I offended you. I hope it's not a bad start."

"Not at all. I'm not offended." I truly wasn't offended, and he was cute, so I gave him a good smile.

Fei Fei and Kala were walking over to us, also smiling. Jean walked a few steps behind, talking quietly on her cell phone. Fei Fei and Kala's smiles were no longer shields used as hacksaws, but such smiles that can be caught by freeze-framing videos of people laughing.

"Kala is ordering three of these blouses—one for each of us," said Fei Fei, holding up a gauzy ivory blouse that looked as though it were crumpled up paper. It had tiny white buttons and a collar that was really a long rectangular length of fabric unhemmed at each end, so that when you buttoned up the shirt, you could close the collar by rolling it and knotting it up like a scarf, with its fuzzy ends of un-woven silk threads.

"Jean doesn't get one," Kala interjected gently and jollily.

"Yes, nothing for Jean. It's not really her style. But Kala's ordering one for you in a larger size, on account of your chest and shoulders. We think it will be a great shirt for a grand occasion."

Fei Fei put her arm around Kala's shoulder and gave her a squeeze. Kala let out a weird squeak. The two femmes did not look alike; for starters, their extractions: Fei Fei's was of Taiwanese, and Kala's, Irish. They were not dressed alike either. Kala was wearing a shiny pink sleeveless top with a wide tubular mock turtleneck and matching pedal-pusher pants. She would have looked like a sixties housewife's idea of the future except she was wearing a pair of old black motorcycle boots so beat up they were green. Fei Fei had on slim but not tight black jeans with pewter front button and pocket rivets, its stovepipe legs so long that cuffed up just once, as she had, the hem almost reached her knee. Tucked into the jeans she wore a faded black shirt that appeared to be just a plain black tee until you went up very close to her or accidentally brushed your skin against the cracked silkscreen print of an image of a happy, boyishly handsome bare-chested guy smooching a happy, handsome Dalmatian, with the letters "sublime long beach" printed over their heads. You couldn't see the image because it was printed in black on black fabric, a manufacturer's error. But on Fei Fei's feet were dainty black patent leather pumps with a heel that was modest and low and came to a sharp, tack-like point. Both femmes carried small, precise, black box-shaped handbags like they planned it ahead of time. Neither wore any jewelry. Even if they were both of the same race and ethnicity, their faces would not have resembled one another. But at that moment, if you took the outlines of their faces and smushed them together, the features would not lie on top of each other perfectly but the imagistic dissonance would have a charm that I, at least, found profoundly moving. I wondered if they were really better friends than they let on to the rest of us.

"And this must be . . . ?" Jean asked, pocketing her phone and nodding towards Aaron.

I made introductions all around, leaving out the part that Aaron and I had met on a gay hook-up website that morning. I don't know if Jean, Kala and Fei Fei assumed that Aaron was my afternoon hook-up or a dude from my past, and they didn't ask as we parted. The women headed south; Aaron and I began walking up the hill of Powell Street.

"Your friend, the Caucasian woman. Is she the actress who used to be on *The Bellingham Blues*?"

I was genuinely surprised. "Yes, that's Kala Young Kenney. I'm surprised you know who she is."

"I used to watch the show. Honestly, she wasn't my favorite—too pouty, too coy. But it was a good show."

We were already at the Starbucks, overflowing with

tourists. Aaron touched my arm to turn me towards him.

"How about we just have coffee or tea at my house? It's just up the hill and I think it would be a lot nicer than Starbucks."

"Well . . ."

"I promise, I'm not trying to force you to do anything you don't want to do."

"I know that. I wouldn't let you force me anyway." We both laughed a little. "Yes, let's go," I said.

Aaron was 57 years old. The photograph he posted online looked professional: there was a white man, light lines on his forehead, around his eyes and mouth, looking directly into the camera with an expression that could have been a smile, an expression too ambiguous for a casual snapshot. He was sitting at a sunlit table with a pair of beautiful hands exposed in front of him, fingers interlaced delicately. Those hands were pink, lightly veined and clear in a way his face wasn't. He had full lips, a strong but proportional nose and serious, unlaughing grey eyes. He had a full head of salt-and-pepper hair but it looked to be receding from his forehead. He looked younger in person. He looked leaner, and he moved with surprising bounciness.

"I like your jacket," I said. "I like those elbow patches."

"Thanks. They probably look pretentious."

"No, I like them." I reached out to stroke one elbow patch. "It's leather. It's like, S&M professor."

Aaron laughed a nice laugh. He was dressed sharp too: an immaculate white oxford shirt, faded blue jeans, oxblood leather loafers, and of course, the tweedy blazer with those umber leather elbow patches. Truthfully, the outfit would have looked much better on a different kind of person; in fact, I feel like I'd seen it on the cover of a magazine, on a young black man with waist-length dreads wearing a bunch of thick silver rings and a nose or lip ring.

0o0

JAMIE WAS COMING DOWN TO SAN FRANCISCO TO STAY with me for a couple nights. While he's here, we'd go to Tish's cat's funeral together. I spent the day cleaning my apartment, dusting exposed surfaces with a jaunty little lithe-handled horsehair brush I usually used just for kink, driving Delilah crazy with the Dirt Devil trying to suck up cotton candy balls of her gold hair from visible crevices, spending half of a lint roller on the black velvet of my chairs, and then I got a call from Jamie saying he had booked a room at a boutique hotel in Hayes Valley.

"I thought you were going to stay with me," I said.

"Yeah, but Jean told me that you live in a studio apartment and I thought it would be nicer this way."

I didn't disagree, especially when I went over to the hotel, which was just a few blocks from my house, and saw how sweet it was. I went up to his room and knocked on the door.

"Hey, my beautiful Howzer!"

"Don't call me that," I snapped, with a scowl. "I don't like that."

Jamie smiled a big, irresistible smile and pulled me in

by the arm, spinning my genuine scowl into saucy flirtation. "Aww, OK. Anyway, I'm not going to call you anything when I fuck you." He said this with an intonation that was very faggotty, but it kind of turned me on.

It's weird and sexy when a guy has a funny-looking face attached to a really hot, built body, but that was Jamie. Big sensual features were crammed into a narrow face whose skin was almost sky blue because of his dark, almost black hair, the thick strands going quickly but neatly bald. He had a big brush of a Super Mario Brothers mustache, orange soda-colored, which was, amazingly, undyed, and just like a cartoon, the only red-haired part of his abundant body hair that was otherwise just as dark as on his head but light and almost fluffy. He had clouded blue eyes, quite beady with long translucent lashes that curled up, and thick dark eyebrow hairs sticking out like pins of foliage; pillowy lips. The comic strip funny face was connected to the rest of his body with a thick neck that was also long and willowy. But his body itself was so hard, so fine, and surprisingly heavy. His pecs were hard and molded just right, in fluid proportion with his shoulders and arms and his belly. When Jamie and I first hooked up I was so fucked up that I didn't remember anything about our fucking but I remembered the jolt I felt when my fingertips touched his shoulders and found (under all the soft long hair) they were so densely muscled.

We got out of our clothes pretty quickly and fell into the hotel bed, which looked kind of like a hospital bed, except if all the bars were taken out and painted a very glossy black. Soon I was laying back with my hands behind my head, stretched out all comfy watching Jamie suck my cock. It was kind of funny because he was looking up at me, locking eyes pretty intensely while he sucked. His dense mustache of orange soda fur got tangled up with my thick black bush and made him look like one of those trick drawings that, when you turn it upside down, looks like something else totally but still makes sense.

I think he sensed my giggles coming on because he abruptly stopped sucking and moved as quick as a snake right up to my face, his hard cock bouncing against mine. He kissed me deeply and we lay there kissing and holding each other for a while. I liked his kissing very much (which again, I didn't remember from before) because he didn't kiss like a lot of guys do, wielding their tongue as if in attack or as a medical exploratory tool. Instead, Jamie used his soft full lips a lot more than his tongue, attaching and detaching himself from my own lips in a lulling but momentous kind of rhythm. My lips felt simultaneously all peeled but not raw, and his lips felt like they were swelling even more.

I was getting really turned on now so I stopped and asked, "Do you want to fuck me now?"

Jamie didn't use words; he kept on kissing me; started jacking me off. His grip was firm but not tight, and as he moved that soft fist up and down my slippery cock, he would loosen and tighten in motions that felt almost conscious, as it fit harmonically with our mouths kissing. He let go for a little moment and put his hands on my hips, adjusting me so that our cocks, both flipped up in erection onto our own bellies, rubbed up against each other, underside to underside. We worked our hips into each other, uninterested in adjusting for any kind of penetration, just two hard cocks creating awkward friction; it felt great.

After a while, Jamie pulled my wrist gently towards his cock and said, mid-kiss, "Jerk me off, too."

I did and he did the same to me, and we continued to kiss, more and more passionately as we jerked faster and faster, our grips getting tighter, but the tightness transformed from discomfort into a flighty kind of pain. We were treating each other's cocks like our own, and revealing to one another our private grips, used when alone or lonely, made us feel extra naked, but in a pleasurable way. Was this intimacy?

"I think I'm going to come," I muttered.

"Wait, don't come yet," responded Jamie, pausing his jerking. "Pump me faster. I'm really close."

I did as told and soon, he grunted in a voice much lower than I'd ever heard from him, "OK, I'm ready. Are you?"

I could feel sperm gathered, bubbling near the end of my urethra. I'm sure I was leaking like crazy already. "Yes, yes, just fucking finish me off," I said.

After we came simultaneously, we lay together for a while, not caring to clean up the gluey mess that was drying and webbing our bellies together. I tucked my head into Jamie's furry chest, and he put his arm around my shoulder and held me tight. I wanted to curl up and count his heartbeats, but I didn't curl up; I just counted his heartbeats.

"Did you date girls in high school?" he asked.

I reached up and played with the hair in the valley of his chest. "Yeah, I dated girls. But I mean, you know, I was a ballet dancer so the girls I dated kind of knew they were dating a gay guy, I think."

"Did you lose your virginity to a girl?"

"No," I blushed. "I actually lost it to a guy, a stranger who cruised me in a park."

"But you've had sex with girls?"

"Yeah, only a couple times. How about you?"

"Never, I'm a gold star faggot. I almost lost my virginity to my best friend in high school, who was a girl. But that was the one and only time. We were making out both shirtless, and I was OK with the breasts, I think. But it was almost like, when I had to fuck her, when I looked down and saw the tip of my cock kind of cushioned against her... you know... I felt so repelled, I really knew I was gay."

"Oh, I think vaginas are kind of cute. I have no desire to fuck them anymore, don't get me wrong. But aesthetically."

Jamie laughed out loud. "You are hilarious," he said, and started playing with my hair. "But I think I know how you are. I was really in the closet in high school, and even dated a few girls, fellow nerds, female. All the while, though, I felt horrible about myself. I was still red-headed and freckly, and pimply, this half-Jewish, half-Irish kid, so I got the worst of white person coloring and hair, and on top of it, of course, chronic acne! But girls, they liked me.

"Teenage girls can sense inner turmoil, and they're drawn to that. But I think teenagers in general are less superficial than they seem; they don't really care if you're ugly if you can make them feel good. Which makes sense because teenagers are really kids in stronger, sexy bodies."

I looked at us, our bodies. With my body, I'm the kind of male dancer who has been out of vogue since the 1970s; actually, probably the sixties. I'm not a big jumper or fast spinner, but I have a wicked second position: nobody can fall into nor push out of second as swiftly or sweetly as I can, and I will brag that my turnout is the best in the whole company. My body is naturally on the slimmer side but, because my workout is focused on partnering and being stationary, I have somewhat bulbous arm and leg muscles that don't quite look right with the rest of me. I have short legs and am not quite six feet tall but look it because I have a long torso, which gives me a lower center of gravity than my height would normally give, which in turn allows me to look willowy while rooting myself solid into the floor. I'm built to move alongside a female dancer and lift her up higher than she can go alone. I'm basically a stepladder on wheels with a dick. I'll never get a lot of solos nor adoring teenage groupies, but I'll always be employed, I'll always be needed.

Maybe because, at that time, ballet dancers were discouraged from tattoos (visible ones were almost explicitly taboo), I didn't have a single tattoo. On his whole body, Jamie had just one tattoo: the Hindi figure for "Om" low on the right side of his belly and so deep into the inside of his hip that it was basically on his groin. I could see it because the symmetrical strip of flesh between his lowest rib, going down over his hip bone and to the top of his thigh, was totally hairless. The tattoo was simple, a little large, faded and blurred so it looked more like a nice birthmark.

I didn't have a tattoo or birthmark but I do have a strange-looking groin. My pubic hair starts only a few centimeters above the root of my penis, but the roots extend down to the top of half of my ball sac. The hair itself is also embarrassingly thick and numerous, each hair freakishly long, a good two inches, my pubic bush so thick and long so that when I stand up, even though my penis is average-sized, it looks as though I have no penis at all; you can only see the strawberry head of my circumcised dick.

It was time to get dressed for the cat funeral. Both of us were infected with short fits of the giggles, on the one hand because we were still on a high from our nice sex, but also because of the idea of dressing for a cat funeral, which we were joking about but not at all taking lightly. We were making cat and lesbian jokes but the whole time I felt a shapeless sadness.

Jamie brushed his mustache with an adorable little boar's bristle brush, then pulled on a loose kind of a black linen t-shirt before putting on his underwear, which were a bikini-cut kind of black cotton briefs; the briefs looked brand-new. Then he put on big black linen trousers that looked as if they were made for a circus clown. But by the time he reached for the pants he already had a narrow, heavy, expensive-looking black leather belt in his teeth like some kind of gay samurai, and once he stepped into the trousers and pulled the waistband to his waist he had whipped that belt around through all the belt loops of the pants which no longer looked like a clown costume but very chic and nimble as the speed with which he belted the whole outfit. Over all this he tossed on a black blazer, fresh as cold lemonade, and folded up the cuffs to expose silk lining, pale cream with thin grey broken pinstripes. Then he padded back into the bathroom—on high pink arches, I noticed—to brush and rake product through his hair.

I opened my big favorite oatmeal-colored Good Vibrations tote bag with the iconic masturbating Cubist lady on it and pulled out my own cat funeral outfit: a child-sized Youth Brigade t-shirt with the sleeves sliced off, black with a graphic of a kind of thrasher-hardcore Pippi Longstocking on the front, and a pair of black Balenciaga pants. Kala bought them for me as a late birthday present at Neiman Marcus a few months ago. Or were they an early birthday present? I would be thirty in November, and I'd forgotten whether she had gotten me a birthday present the previous year. These were technically women's pants, and the fabric was a heavy kind of nylon—barely stretchy but flexible like women's swimsuits—and weighed a ton. The way you got into them was by opening a zipper that ran on the left side from the knee all the way to the waist. I don't wear these pants too often because of this: I have to unzip the big side zipper almost to my knee to be able to get my dick out to take a piss, and if I'm in a public restroom, I feel shy about exposing so much of myself to the pisser to my left. This big zipper had thick plastic teeth that reminded you of children's bumbling fingers, and a big-ass metal pull that was so ridiculous in proportion that you were forced to look at it like a very fancy earring. There were also much tinier zippers, very dainty, that crawled all over the legs—over the knees, on the sides of the thighs, around the shin and calves and ankles—each anchored to teensy teardrop-shaped metal tabs that were lacquered limousine-black. When you put them on, the small zipper tabs all converged at the insides of your thighs and swung with their unexpectedly heavy weight, hitting each other and making the tiniest music.

The big side zip was already open, so I turned the pants upside down and undid the teensy zippers at the ankles so I could put my feet into them. I sat at the foot-edge of the bed and put my feet through and pulled the zips up when I remembered that I hadn't unzipped the knees yet. At Neiman's, when I was trying the pants on, I put my feet through and just pulled them up by the waist; the pants got caught on my big calves and knees and as I gave a little yank, I heard a distinct ripping sound.

"Eek," I turned to Kala, feeling like a caught shoplifter. "Maybe I should get a bigger size. I hope it didn't rip."

"I think that sounded like a rip," Kala said casually and came over to inspect. "I don't see anything on the outside. Maybe you tore some stitches from the seams or something. It doesn't matter anyway, we'll most likely buy this pair. This is the right size for you—it's supposed to fit skintight. If it sags or wrinkles it will look wrong. Here, unzip the knees."

She was right; then they pulled up like magic, or like I was greased up. I unzipped the knees now and then pulled them right up and just over my navel, then pulled up the big side zipper, but I pulled a little too fast and it pinched the skin at my side.

Jamie heard me squeak from the pinch just as he was coming out of the bathroom.

"Hey, you look great," he said, and studied me as I zipped up the knees. "I can see the puffy outline of your pubic hair through those. Really sexy. Sexy enough for the funeral of a cat of a good friend."

"Thanks," I said soberly as I put on my little t-shirt. I didn't bring any product for my hair. I don't like the feeling of tacky hair and I only use product for work. I shook out my damp hair and let the long pieces in the front stab my cheeks and bits of eyeball, then put on my glasses.

"Are those glasses real?"

"Yes," I answered, not too soberly. "Reach out and touch. You are not imagining them."

"Ha. You know what I mean. Do you need them to see?"

"As it happens, yes, I need them to see. I'm a little near-sighted, or is it far-sighted, I don't remember which is which. I can't read signs that are far away. I need them to drive but since I don't have a car, and I can still dance without them, I don't wear them most of the time. But I felt like wearing them today." My glasses were round, thin rims of golden wire.

"I'm glad you need them. It's stupid to wear fake glasses."

I didn't think it was that stupid, but I didn't say anything.

"Are you ready?" Jamie asked as he pulled on thin black silk socks and laced up immaculate black oxfords. It was impressive how he was wearing many pieces of black clothing and they were all exactly the same shade of black—not one in the bunch that was sun- or detergent-faded.

"Just my shoes, but they're over by the door and I just have to slip them on, obviously."

"Oh, you didn't bring any shoes?"

"Those are shoes."

"No, they are sandals. Actually, they're not that either. They are Tevas."

Jamie cocked his head and pouted contemplatively. Without the pout, he would have reminded me of Delilah when she hears me making a sound she doesn't recognize.

"Well," I continued as I walked over to the shoes—I mean, the Tevas. "They're black."

"Hold on," Jamie said. He came over and stood very close to me. He was a couple inches shorter than me and smelled clean but fragrant. He unhooked the bracelet he was wearing on his right wrist; I hadn't noticed until now that he was left-handed. He held it up in front of me like it was a hypnotist's chain-watch or the shot-dead water snake of a Louisiana redneck. The bracelet was made of gold links, thin as sewing thread. I saw that there were a couple wavy hairs caught along its length; although he unclasped it with his usual delicacy, Jamie had pulled it from his wrist with a bit of savagery.

"Put this on," he said.

I took the bracelet and softly slapped it on my left wrist.

"No, put it on your ankle. Here, let me."

He took the bracelet back, knelt down in the pose of a nostalgic suitor, and clasped the bracelet around my right ankle. I imagined him looking at the place beside and under my ankle bone, where the skin is extra pale and thin, where overworked blood vessels pumped blood so hard that it made this small area palpitate hard fast shudders all the time, as if it had its own pink little heart.

"Now you will look beautiful," he declared, beaming up into my face. The way he said that, in words and tone so stiff and formal, sounded as if he were a rich foreigner practicing English in America.

Down in the lobby, Jamie had the concierge call us a cab and then we were on our way to Russian Hill. Tish lives a couple blocks just west of Van Ness, so I think it's technically not Russian Hill, but her condo is the top floor of a gorgeous Victorian that looks like a wedding cake, painted in three different shades of white, with a view of the Marina that always looks like a painted backdrop in an old movie. The weather was predictably nippy outside and of course I knew better, but there I was, shivering sweaterless in a little tee with the sleeves cut out, a hem that only covered half of my belly, sitting in pants that allowed no distance between it and my body. My tote bag was sitting on the puffy new-vintage armchair back in Jamie's hotel room, holding only the sweats I wore to meet him. The bouquet of faded-orange tea roses I bought for Tish was on my lap. My keys and wallet were nesting in the interior pocket of Jamie's coat; he promised to take me back to my house to feed and walk Delilah after we were done at Tish's.

Honestly, I didn't know what to expect from the cat funeral. I'd never been to a funeral for a pet, although I've been to enough memorial services for people who died of AIDS. Actually, when Tish had said "funeral" I heard "memorial service" ("meow-morial service," Jamie had quipped) because I assumed we wouldn't be witnessing an actual burial (Tish didn't have a yard) nor cremation in her living room, which I hoped was true because I had never witnessed the actual burial of any dead person or animal and I didn't know if I could take it. Those three memorial services I'd been to had been, in keeping with the times, simply and importantly, celebrations of lives lived. One was a jumbled and silly color-laden dance party, another was more traditionally somber but featured a beautiful classical music quartet, and the last was a midnight gathering in the valley of Dolores Park featuring glitter-decorated Ziploc baggies of mushrooms and jam jars of homemade absinthe. They were truly laughter-and-tears kind of moments. Being a gay male person, AIDS scared me, of course, but less so now than ten years ago, when it scared me to death. And these gatherings had helped: helped me think more about my inside parts as complicated and interestingly inscrutable rather than something inevitably vulnerable that had to be vigilantly bulwarked against virus or sex. The lesson of the dead was also a lesson about death, which was to remember to never live in fear, as long as you were living. I was just a kid during the really high bell curve of AIDS deaths in the 1980s, but even I have personally known three people—two guys, one girl; all three just a few years older than me—who died of AIDS and I think three is plenty: for me, for anybody, really. On the other hand, I personally know a ton of people, all gay men, including Jamie, who are HIV positive, and while that statistical fact is nothing to celebrate, knowing them and seeing them live their lives with brave nonchalance, their bodies in a wide range of physical states from weak to stronger than my HIV negative self, that doesn't make me sad at all.

I half expected to walk in and see a small coffin, its lid put aside, inlaid with red velvet cake-colored velvet, with Squirrel nestling within. That was Tish's cat's name—Squirrel. She named him that because, even as a kitten, he had a weird big bushy tail that didn't seem at all feline, and then, after jokingly calling him that for a few days, she grew to like the feeling of the sound that made in her mouth; she said it made her feel like she was purring along with him. I didn't know him as a kitten but as an adult, Squirrel was a big, fat, indolent, sloppy, nasty cat. But like a lot of nasty cats, he was gorgeous, long plush silver-blue fur dotted here and there with gold. Even at rest, his fur stood up in thick peaks like meringue, and when he got pissed, it all unfurled into whirls and swirls. His snout was on the long side for a cat, so sometimes, at certain jolting angles he almost looked like some squashed-face dogs. I'm not much of a cat person to begin with, but I knew Squirrel to be both mean and beautiful.

A long time ago, this was before I adopted Delilah, I stayed with Squirrel for five days while house- and cat-sitting for Tish. For the first couple days, Squirrel acted the stereotypical cat; he did his thing around his home not caring or noticing that his owner was not there. I was just a pulsing dispenser of food and occasional rubs, and I was fine with that; like I said, I'm indifferent to cats so his indifference didn't hurt my feelings. But on the third day, I came home from work and found little piles of hard pebble-poop and puddles of piss all over the apartment: under the sofa in the difficult nook between the ledge of the seat and the delicate leg, smack-dab middle under the kitchen table, at the foot of the bed, in the bathtub, on the little hook rug right by the entrance. I had a particularly shitty and humiliating day in class and rehearsal so this situation made me angry, especially as Squirrel was otherwise his normal self, prowling about with mysterious purpose and hogging the pretty little sofa. As I finished cleaning up, wiping up an especially wide spread of smelly urine under the mantle, Squirrel suddenly leapt off the sofa and sauntered over to me and mewed: loud, gurgling, piercing meow. I looked down and saw he was rubbing his head against my calf. I don't know what came over me but I muttered something like "Oh you asshole," and I kicked him away. I didn't do it hard, and it wasn't a kick exactly—as he rubbed, I pushed my leg against him and pulled back quickly so Squirrel was caught off balance and got knocked up and down, like half a foot. But it felt like I kicked him because he was clearly startled, and ran away to the bathroom. He stayed there the rest of the evening and I felt so bad, I kept trying to coax him back to the bedroom but he wouldn't come, just stared at me, blinking. I never told Tish about this and come to think of it, I never told it to anyone; to think of it now, even, makes me feel a tremendous kind of shame.

There was no coffin with Squirrel in it. Women were moving about the room without any noticeable solemnity, but a little more slowly than normal. There was music: when we entered I could make out strains of the Pretenders' "Don't Get Me Wrong," but it was playing so softly it was emptied of any swag and fun. Then it switched to a song I didn't know, by a band I didn't recognize, but full of murderous jangling guitars and fast drums and a male voice spitting that I knew was never meant to be played at this soft volume, even though it gave the song a kind of heart you might have missed if you were sweating and pushing fast with it. The women were dressed in normal clothes—there was no plethora of black clothes, although of course, a lot of people just wear black clothes every day, and the black there didn't seem out of the ordinary, neither formal nor sad. Most of the women were wearing pants, either as part of a suit or with a button-down shirt, and some with vests. I spotted Fei Fei at the other end of the room by the window, talking to a butch I didn't know in a grey vest and pink shirt. From the entryway where I stood with Jamie (the little hook rug long gone), it looked as though Fei Fei was wearing a strange black suit: narrow trousers cropped at the ankles and a collarless double-breasted jacket that came to a fast point at the waist, then blew out again around the hips, so that her torso looked as though it belonged to a fat woman who had been laced into a tiny little fetish corset. When I finally found my way to her later, I saw that it wasn't a suit at all, but a thin black sweater worn under a bustier made of black wool.

The room felt like a normal semiformal party. Voices weren't at all muted; there was a variety of loudness and animation in conversations that I could hear were both serious and gossipy; there was laughter. The music went to Anita Baker's "No One in the World," and I heard Tish's voice say, "Oh, turn that up. All the way up, Lee, please!" Anita Baker played at thrash-metal volume was quite swinging.

Tish, like the other women, looked formal but not abnormally so. Tish is a lawyer, so whenever we hang out—whether at a dinner party or coffee after the gym—I think she'll show up in a suit. Of course that's not the case, but tonight she was wearing a suit, a narrow-cut suit in a shade of white I had never seen before: when she moved, it seemed to turn almost yellow. She was wearing a lavender kind of ribbed tank top instead of a blouse. Tish is African-American, and the particular lavender of the top was particularly flattering to her skin tone. Because she left the jacket open, I could see that the suit was lined in a richly bronze silk printed with dark abstract blobs. I handed her the flowers.

"I'm so sorry, Tish," I said.

"Oh, thanks Howie. How lovely these are. Thank you. Squirrel would have loved them."

I had an image of tough, fat Squirrel shredding the poor roses to bits just for the hell of it and walking away, remorseless, slaughter instantly forgotten as always. Tish did not sound like herself. She didn't sound sad exactly, and moreover, she was smiling slightly. But her voice was pitched a smidge higher than usual, and she spoke in a weird intonation, as though inside herself, she were silently counting something only she could see. It made me think of a priestess in an ancient cult, and also the one time I was hired to do pop-dance work, a comeback music video for dance music diva who had been semi-famous in the '70s, a diminutive woman with a charmingly doughy face who was in great shape and actually a great, intuitive dancer, who snap-clap-vogued with and dressed exactly the same (black flamenco blouse, black stretch pants, black boas made of fabric 'feathers,' strange white Mary Jane shoes with huge rubber platform soles) as 20 back-up dancers male and female, so that she looked as if she were lip-synching her cutely wobbly bass trip-hop-inflected nu-disco song in a black hall of mirrors.

"I think you know Jamie?" I said.

She looked at him, smile unchanged; clearly she didn't.

"Hi Tish. I'm a friend of Jean's. She and I went to high school together. I think we met a couple years ago at her sister's house?"

Tish nodded. "Thanks so much for coming, Jamie." I still wasn't sure if she remembered him, and she wasn't either, I think.

"I never knew Squirrel, but Jean told me he was a beauty," Jamie said, and looked vaguely around, as if looking for Squirrel himself but more likely, some photograph or image of him.

"Oh yes, he was a beauty, but he could also be an asshole. But he was beautiful so he could be an asshole," she said.

We—including Tish—nodded. I asked her: "Where is Squirrel? Did you have him buried or cremated?"

"He's been cremated. He's in that box, there on the mantle." She pointed across the room and sure enough, there was a medium-sized box of red, shellacked wood sitting placidly on the white mantle. "And also in here." She reached into her jacket pocket and revealed a teensy silver box, oblong-shaped and black with oxidation. She shook the box near my ear as if it were a musical instrument and indeed it made a slightly irritating noise of clink and hiss.

"Bone," she said, and put the box back in her pocket. "I have to fly to Kentucky tomorrow for work and I can't bear to be away from Squirrel just yet. I know it's morbid."

Neither Jamie nor I contradicted nor affirmed her morbidity. I was busy listening to the memory of the leftover bone of Squirrel, and looked over again towards the mantle at the red box. It was shining, still and omniscient as Buddha but totally naïve, oblivious. I burst into tears. I thought about the toe bone or the tip of the tail bone of Squirrel sloshing with a tablespoon of his ashes as his former owner moved through airport security, in and out of hotels and taxis. Squirrel had been 15 years old when he died. In the last year or so of his life, Squirrel developed cancerous tumors all around his face. They were huge and not at all pink and fleshy as you might expect but instead grey and leaden: metallic, almost. Arranged around his face in a nonsense pattern—a small cluster next to his left eye, a bigger one next to his right nostril, another cluster dotting his lips so that the sharp teeth were totally hidden even when bared—the tumors looked like baubles of avant-garde adornment. They might have been ungainly on another cat, but being as big and fat as he was, Squirrel carried them around with the stoicism of the fashionable.

Through my tears I could see next to the red box a tiny wrought-iron picture frame, and because I knew the frame, I knew that it held a snapshot of Squirrel as a kitten. I knew that Tish had cut a passport-sized rectangle around Squirrel from a regular-sized photo of her ex-girlfriend holding him. In this photo, Squirrel is a totally different cat: a little punk rock, his nose and mouth look little but longing, and he's skinny. His eyes are wide and dark as a beagle's, scared but on the precipice of happiness, too. His head seems vulnerable, huge and bobbing over a delicate neck, his ribbon-thin red collar cutting into grey fur that hasn't yet gained the shine of years of indulgence and canned carnage.

My tears kept coming, and between sobbing in the way in which tears and snot become indistinguishable, I asked Tish: "Why are you going to Kentucky, of all places?"

Tish replied as if I weren't blubbering, and for that I was grateful. "I'm going to do some consulting work for a public defender I know in Lexington. It's such a beautiful city—horses literally everywhere. But my friend the public defender has got this client who is a sex worker, female, who has a felony charge of, quote, 'prostitution while infected with HIV.' She could get up to five years in prison for giving her john—an undercover cop, mind you—a hand job."

"Oh my god," Jamie said. "A hand job?"

"Yes," said Tish. "He came in her hand and then arrested her. Of course he denies orgasming."

"But . . . you can't give someone HIV by masturbating them!"

"Yes, but in the magic land of Kentucky you can," explained Tish, her tone still unchanged, still counting something invisible. "You'd be surprised how many states have the same kind of criminal code."

"I didn't even know having HIV could be a crime," I said.

"That's exactly it," Tish said. She had got rid of her smile. I wasn't sure if it was from the infuriating stupidity of laws or the thought of a baby Squirrel. "But they call it 'transmission' or 'exposure,' even when there is no intimate contact or exchange of fluids, or only exchange of fluids that can't transmit HIV. You can get arrested for assault if you have HIV and spit at a cop. Some states call it 'assault with bodily fluids' or just 'bioterrorism.' In Indiana, included in the category of such dangerous body fluids is tears."

0o0

AFTER THE THIRD TIME WE HAD BEEN TOGETHER, Aaron wanted me to fuck him. All three times we'd been at his place, and I'd never spent the night.

"You're ravishing. I'm not handsome," Aaron said. I would have blushed and felt pleasure at the compliment but for what he said about himself. He was naked, and I didn't think he was not handsome; it's just he was the kind of man who looks truly handsome only when not smiling. I was naked too. I approached and kissed him fully and for a good while as we stood together. Our tongues were in each other's mouths, I ran my hands all over him, making a tactile map of his body. His neck had two thick veins, symmetrically positioned from beneath his chin to the tops of his clavicles, just under skin that had become thin, delicate, and striated, and was quite thick where it attached to his shoulders, but got narrower as it merged up to his rather small head, giving the idea of a stereotypical tree. The skin of his neck felt the same as that of his hands, where you could see the veins under skin, the color of white skin that's been in the bath too long, and covered with hatchings in familiar patterns, checkers and waves. His wrists were ringed with deep grooves as if he'd just been released from tight bondage. I knew by this time that those hands were great all over me. With age he had lost most of his body hair that must have been thick and wavy at some time but now thin and grey, and on his forearms, there was no hair at all. His arms were a bit scaly and dotted with almost totally white patches. They were still pretty strong, even though they looked a bit slight attached to a torso that looked stocky. He was lean all over except his midsection, which gave away his age. His belly was hard with muscle, but I couldn't find a true waist; there was just enough permanent fat all around to make his stomach look just like it was pulled stretched straight down from his chest rather than carefully stacked segments of flesh upon the vulnerable stomach and intestines. My hands rested on that solid but weirdly helpless waist.

"I'm just now, at 57, only OK-looking," he told me. "As a young man, I knew I was ugly. But you know, as a child, I was beautiful. Look, I'll show you a photo; it will be proof. Then you'll feel better because even though you're fucking a mediocre-looking old man, you'll know that you've also been fucking someone who used to be a beautiful child."

We put our kiss on pause and Aaron walked over to pluck a photograph from the top of his bedroom dresser, the surface of which was as broad as a museum showcase. The snapshot was caught in a thick expensive frame, and when I held it, it looked and felt as heavy as lead.

"This is you," I said.

"Yes," he confirmed.

The snapshot looked old, and its age was shimmery. A child in bathing trunks, smiling a half-moon grin full of pale baby teeth and black baby gaps, a smile that should have led with the chin but because it was tucked in, made the boy look quite shy as he sat at the edge of a swimming pool, sticking his toes up out of the water in an awkward but cute way, his hair all wet and sticking out all over. The expression of the kid's face was made touching by the big polished picture frame, which made the boy seem even smaller, his shy face even shyer than it may have really been.

The picture was one among a few on the dresser top, and I'm sure I'd seen it before as I grazed over Aaron's apartment, making a grid of my appreciation of his wealth. But funny how I'd never noticed this. It made me wonder how drunk we'd both been the two previous times we had hooked up. Or fucked up: Aaron liked his cocaine and in fact just had had a line now. The vision of the line of coke on the nightstand made me think about Jamie, how I hadn't known that he was AA sober until much later. I had been so fucked up at the bar that first night in Healdsburg that I assumed that Jamie, too, had been drinking; only later he revealed that he had been drinking ginger ale.

"OK now I'm going to fuck you as you requested," I said, and spun Aaron around and pushed him gently on the edge of the bed, where he maneuvered himself up to the ledge, ass high in the air. He had a sweet deep dimple on each butt cheek. I parted him with my hands and observed his asshole. It was pink and tender, and surrounded by beige and grey curls that straightened out as it moved out from the hole to the soft skin of the insides of his butt. I was surprised by the sumptuousness of his asshole hair, because of his age and also he trimmed his pubic hair down almost to stubbles—which I didn't like—and even shaved his balls. I made a mental note to ask him later about why he didn't shave or trim his asshole. I pressed my lips to it as if it were a mouth, feeling through the thick bush the warm moist hole. I kissed it chastely, quickly and repeatedly until Aaron's moans transformed from sound to vibrations folded many times to fit into the space between his bones and skin. I stuck my tongue in. My tongue isn't very pointy and it's not particularly dexterous so I think my tongue-fucking wasn't getting him off as much as my kissing the outer regions of his rectum. But he was wet enough now for me to finger-fuck him so I did that a little bit. My hands are big but I have thin fingers so I began right away with both my index and middle finger, my thumb cocked like I was a kid playing "Cowboys-and-Indians," but I always wanted to subvert the midcentury racism of the game by acting out the "Indian" who slings out a surprise musket and blows dumb "Cowboy" away. My head and torso were a notable distance from his ass that allowed me to watch and study my own fingers as they were fucking him, which made the whole thing feel a little clinical. My palm rubbed the inside of his butt as I fucked him like this for a while, then I rotated my wrist, added my ring finger and fucked him in the traditional style, palm up, fingers petting his prostate. Like this, I fucked him a bit longer and kept watching my arm move toward and away from his damp, jacked-up butt.

With my left hand, I reached under and felt his smooth ball sac, and then his cock. He was hard, so as I fucked him, I jacked him off a little, but only a little, because the position was awkward and hurt my wrist. When I felt like he was sufficiently prepared, I pulled out my fingers and patted his butt reassuringly with my left hand while I hobbled over to the nightstand to get a condom. I was really hard by this time: my piss slit heavy with precum.

“Please, keep fucking me with your fingers right up until you fuck me,” Aaron murmured.

I obliged him and opened the condom, the pinked edge of its gold foil wrapper between my big teeth. I ripped it open nimbly, and standing there behind Aaron, my fingers moving into his butthole, rubber-wrapper in my teeth, I felt embarrassingly like cheesy porn. In that spirit, I spat out the wrapper carelessly onto the bed before rolling the rubber onto my cock and placing the wrapped cock into Aaron.

I fucked him soft, soft, hard, hard, hard, soft, hard, soft, soft, soft, so that when I was close he could feel it even though I couldn’t help saying, “Shit I’m close.” During the second hard sequence he wanted us to change positions so we could kiss while fucking; I refused.

“Maybe another time. Today—just like this,” I said.

Finally, I pulled out, peeled out of the condom and sprayed Aaron’s animal backside with my cum. He was busy jacking himself off, still on his knees.

"Put yourself back in me," he said with irresistible desperation.

"No," I answered. The tip of my cockhead was still gobby with sperm and I didn't want that in him. As he continued to work his cock, Aaron reached over with his left and began to fuck himself with his middle finger, rhythmically massaging his asshole too. I reached over and held his cock while he turned his hips in order to come.

Eventually Aaron cleaned the tip of my penis with his mouth, then relaxed back against the pillows and we lay side by side.

"Do you want to stay the night tonight?" he asked.

I thought about the possible reasons for never having spent the entire night with him. I didn't want things to get too serious. I felt things were too serious so I didn't want to set myself up for failure. I didn't think either of those thoughts were true. Then I wondered if the reason I never stayed the night with him was because of Delilah: she needed me to give her food, to walk her, let her relieve her bladder and bowels because in her pattern of life and self, what we humans condescendingly call "conditioning," she felt it, in the cells of her body, impossible to soil the worthless wood boards and linoleum she spent most of her time upon. But that still didn't explain why I never felt the need or desire to invite him over to my place—not that he asked to come over, either. Because I wanted to maintain a certain image of myself to him, which was what? And why did I even care? Because Aaron's place was so much more luxurious and not cramped?

He had an actual bed, a four-poster, mattress at perfect hip height so I could properly fuck him standing with my legs spread out like poles at outdoor camp, my butt muscles spasmic and his tremulous butthole dovetailing into the trimming of thousand thread-count Egyptian cotton? Fucking like this made us feel like stupid, simple machines made of mushy disposable stuff, while the great dark carved bed stood still with its pillar-legs, its carved surface with grooves as numerous and fine as fur.

"Yeah. I think I do," I said. "But I have to call my friend Val... we have a date to go late-night jogging together..."

Aaron raised his eyebrow. "Val? You have a date with someone?"

"Val is a dyke, a woman. Anyway, my dog needs to be taken out and walked. I could pop over in a couple hours to do all that, and come right back?"

"How about you break your date with Val, and get a neighbor or friend who can take care of the dog for you. I would really like us to go out for dinner, some place nice, and have a proper evening together."

"OK."

Aaron let out a big sigh of what sounded like relief or ecstasy, and lay on my breastbone. He lay carefully, making sure not to make dead weight of his head against what he must have surely, accurately, divined was a delicate bone of a delicate person. We stayed like this for a while, and it felt nice, although I was trying to think of who I should call to take care of Delilah, and also if it was a good idea for her to spend the whole night all alone in the apartment. Aaron didn't offer anything like: "Bring her over, I love dogs."

"Why don't you ever talk about your family?" Aaron suddenly asked.

"I do. I've told you about Fei Fei, and Jean, and . . ."

"I understand that your friends are your family, your chosen family, all of that queer politics. Remember, I was actually alive in the '60s. I mean your parents, where you come from."

I didn't answer, and instead picked at my pubes, plucking fuzz and breaking apart dried cum that had stuck the hairs together in clumps. For some reason, when I saw Val later that night, I didn't mention the photograph of Aaron as a child even though I did say to her these exact words: "I didn't feel like answering him, I just picked at my pubes, plucking fuzz and breaking dried cum apart from hairs stuck together in clumps."

Aaron's BlackBerry started ringing in the middle of my silence. He rolled over off me and reached over to the bedside table to pick up. He said Hello in a somewhat robotic voice that melted quickly into an effusive laughter, and he visibly relaxed into the phone and the brief conversation, in which he told whoever it was at the other end to come over.

"Ivor's coming over," Aaron said as he got up and started towards the bathroom.

Suddenly, I was alone in bed, dust of drying cum all about me, my legs splayed out in front of me like a rag doll. I could hear his shower running. I would have gotten up, to clean myself up as well, but somehow, I didn't feel like the moment felt right to follow him into the bathroom for a romantic couples shower. Instead I yelled out from where I stayed, "Who is Ivor?"

I pulled myself up to a more sitting position and shifted into a different kind of silence. Aaron finally came back, a thick grey towel wrapped around his waist, and his wet hair had been combed.

"Did you say something?"

"Who is Ivor?" I repeated lightly.

"Oh, Ivor. Ivor is my assistant."

I didn't move, just looked at him a smidge hard. "It's just that the way you said 'Ivor is coming over,' sounded like I should know who he is, and of course, I have no idea who he is."

"Oh, really? I didn't mean it that way. I'm doing a free-lance article for *W* magazine on these ritzy seaside towns between Los Angeles and the Bay Area, and he's been helping me compile and organize research that I really need tonight, so he's going to bring them over, that's all."

Aaron was smiling, and his voice was normal, and maybe it was the very normality of it all, but I felt like I had just stolen something really huge and heavy and he was letting me leave with it.

"You didn't say you had to work. Should I go after all?"

"No, no, stay. He's going to drop the stuff off and that's it." Aaron opened his closet and started thumbing through his shirts, eventually pulling out a soft white button-down.

I went into the bathroom and took a shower. As soon

as I turned the water off, I heard Aaron call out my name.

I toweled off and went naked into the kitchen where he was calling. Ivor was there. Seeing me without any clothes on, both of them began to giggle.

"Howie, meet Ivor. Ivor, Howie."

There stood a short young man, with a lovely face in which everything was almond-shaped: eyes, full lips, even his soft nose was an almond held up vertically to look like a teardrop. He had kind of reddish light brown hair that looked professionally dyed, cut tidily and shaped with gel. He was dressed in a shirt in multicolored stripes that were subtle rather than garish, perfectly faded pressed denim jeans, and hard-looking leather shoes. On the floor next to the iron-worked barstool from which he got up was one of those large canvas tote bags from Lands' End or J.Crew, stiff and square as a packing box, with handle and trim in an obnoxious shade of green, and on the front, same green initials done in preppy embroidery: "I M I." He was of Asian descent.

"Hello," Ivor said, and extended his hand.

"Hi Ivor," I said, and took it with a small smile. He shook my hand with a grip that was really hard. I suppose it was meant to signal masculinity or some such shit, but it honestly it just really hurt. Being naked, I just looked a little down at him, which was easy enough as he was almost a head shorter than me.

There was a long pause, and Aaron spoke. I had forgotten he was even in the room.

"Hey, Ivor brought over this delicious pork adobo and

I thought I'd whip up some noodles to go with it. Do you want a snack, Howie?"

I smiled wider, with teeth. Ivor was smiling too, but chin down, more like a kind of smirk.

"No, thanks. I really should get going," I said.

"Oh really? Stay and have some of this with us. It's really good. Ivor's a terrific cook," said Aaron in a voice that was almost sing-song. I was getting a little dizzy from all the whirling significations of "us."

"My mom's the terrific cook, and she taught me everything," Ivor said as he resumed his seat at the counter and put one hand lightly on a big blue Tupperware box that, I assumed, held said adobo.

"Thanks, Aaron. And Ivor. But also I don't eat meat. I don't know if you remember that, Aaron."

I could hear Aaron say something like "Oh yeah . . ." as I turned and went back into the bedroom to collect my clothes. In the shower I had noticed that I lost my tiny little silver nose piercing. That wasn't unusual because it's just a like a shaving of a staple, a thin little hook of pure silver, made to sit hookside in among my nostril hairs, and which from the outside looked like I just had a little speck of silver dust on a nostril pore, perfect for a dancer who not only can't have visible body piercings but has to be wary of things getting snagged by partner's hair or leotard or tights or shoe ribbon. The piercing was so small it was always getting lost and often not found. As I picked up my clothes from the bedroom floor I knew the little hook was somewhere down there. I thought: Let them step on it and pierce the soft toe underside or the edge of the ball of their foot. I had a few more back at home and besides, my metalsmith friend who made it would always send me more. I looked at the clock on the dresser top: it was 7:45.

By 9:30 I was back home, Delilah fed and walked, and I was getting into my jogging clothes, which was just an old pair of black nylon swimming trunks and a t-shirt so beat up so badly it could pass for ultrabreathable moisture-wicking polyester. It said: "Colorado Ballet." I laced up my running shoes, leashed Delilah in her special "hands-free" lead, and went outside to wait for Val, who was supposed to pick me up a little before ten. She arrived at 9:56.

Val and I had learned that we both liked to jog at night, so we promised we'd go together sometime, with Delilah as well. I only run during the summer months between seasons, because I actually have time. In season, I have to get up early, be in class or rehearsal basically until evening, by which time, if I don't have a performance, I just want to sack out with a book, guy, or drink. I don't like to get up too early if I don't have to, and I hate jogging in the streets, swerving to avoid people, so I like to go at night. Val suggested she drive us over to the Richmond to try an especially rad route.

"There are some amazingly calm blocks west of Clement," she had said enthusiastically. "Broad and marvelous slow incline that just sneaks up on you just so. We can jog right up to the entrance of the Legion of Honor, then around the VA hospital and come out of the park triumphantly high atop the corner near the Cliff House!"

Val drove some kind of a long hatchback number, green but not obnoxiously green. It was almost teal, with a lot of douchebag-like silver trimming, but with Val behind the wheel, it looked cool. She kept it very clean except the rear window, which was really dirty, and in the grime someone had written: "PLEASE WASH ME, PLEASE!!"

"Usually I keep this car pretty spotless, except I had to go back and tend to some family business back east and while I was gone someone wrote that on the rear window. I kept it when I cleaned the car because don't you think the handwriting is quite good? It's really inspirational. I'll clean it as soon as I remember to take a good picture of it."

I had to admit, the handwriting was pretty good—solid and curvy at the same time. Then I told Val about my interlude with Aaron and Ivor.

"Do you think he really was his assistant? Or was that his boyfriend?" Val asked.

"I honestly don't know. It felt like, yeah, his assistant. And Aaron and I hadn't even talked about a relationship or anything—I mean, I certainly didn't mention that I was in the market for a boyfriend or anything—so why should he hide the fact of having a boyfriend?"

"Well, people are weird sometimes, especially fags. Not that I know from personal experience, but from personal experience of knowing quite a few of them, they tend to assume your feelings about them before you tell them what you feel about them. Sorry to stereotype."

"That's OK. I think you're probably right. I mean, I

probably did or do that myself. But the weird thing about tonight was, something really bothered me that Ivor was Asian. I hate saying that out loud. It makes me feel like one of those pathetic self-hating Asians who see competition rather than . . ."

"Brotherhood?"

"Ick, god no. Camaraderie?"

Val, Delilah, and I jogged by the light of a dainty moon. It was hard to tell what shape or phase it was beneath all the clouds, but clouds look white even in the dark night of this particular stretch of Richmond so it didn't feel gloomy at all. Actually, it reminded me of when I first moved to San Francisco, and I would spend those precious free days before actual work walking all over the city. Compared to where I came from, the city felt conjoined with the atmosphere. What I mean is—the air and the ground felt like the same thing. Your foot hitting the hilly concrete felt the same as your sinuses and lungs filling with air filled with leftover fog, and it all felt wonderful. Even the Richmond at night, which is much more residential than other parts of San Francisco, still felt the same as SoMa or Valencia or the Castro. A city of anorexic, supermodel white churches, pastel ice cream sandwich houses (so much salmon paint!), trees like ratty charming wigs on stilty stands.

I say we "jogged" because we weren't at all running, but technically we weren't really walking, either. But our knees were lifting high and the soles of our feet floated occasionally. This was because Val and I were chatting as we ran, and also because of Delilah. Lately I've been catching myself training concentrated gaze upon her backside in motion. Because of her ethnicity, as a German Shepherd, I knew that hip dysplasia was coming hard for her some day. So far it had been manageable but ever since she turned six years old in February I began to spend more time looking into my dog's face and seeing a misfitting hip bone slowly pulverizing its partner socket. I knew some humans, all female, all ballet dancers, all older, who had problems with their hips because of dysplasia, but in their case the dysplasia was not a sign of deterioration but source of longevity; it was dysplasia that allowed them to be ballet dancers and a few, great dancers because the weird small sockets that give a German Shepherd an uncomfortable, wobbly gait and eventual pain is what allows the human to kick and turn out in the abnormal angles that become art. When I think that German Shepherds are bred to have dysplasia, their sad, elegant slumped down hindquarters, I think maybe Delilah is closer to the dysplasiac women than she is to me.

Delilah was her original name. When she was four years old, she was surrendered by her original owner, who had raised her all her life, to the no-kill shelter in Santa Barbara, where I got her. This original owner was an old man who had worked for years in Hollywood providing and training animal actors, especially dogs. Delilah was his last dog. From a cinematic distance, she looked like a pure German Shepherd Dog. But when you went round and looked into her face, you knew she was a mix with something else, most probably equal parts

Labrador, Golden Retriever, and Beagle. The proportion of her eyes and snout and nose was very Beagley. Unlike most GSD's, she didn't have black fur on her snout and eye area. In fact, because of that, the man would regularly paint her face black with a nontoxic vegetable dye. Except once, she was powdered up like the 18th century to play a wolf in a western. Her owner was an elegant man in his eighties wearing a signet pinky ring and subtly gleaming black Adidas tracksuit, trimmed in deep magenta. He had decided to retire and move to Atlanta to live with someone who was a cat person and hated dogs. He looked defeated when he surrendered Delilah, but not sad. Delilah was frightened and depressed, but the man had not cried. He only said: "She's a beautiful animal. I just can't let them keep making her owned by Nazis and the police. You know she was in that movie with Alec Baldwin about the murdered civil rights workers, and they made her chase black kids down. I just hope nothing of that went into her, and stayed with her. I just hope that."

The day I went to the shelter and fell in love with Delilah, it just so happened that the person who processed her surrender was working, and was able to tell me her whole story. He was a skinny guy, with pitted cheeks and hair dusted with dandruff but carefully greased and combed, who looked older than he probably was—and he looked like he was in his late forties. I noticed he had a lot of shitty, blurred tattoos on his arms and fingers, and he was missing a few teeth inside a cruel thin mouth. But his eyes looked kind and fatigued, and he spoke to Delilah in the same tone as he did to me, rather than the high-pitched exaggerated babyspeech used by the other workers, so I figured he was OK and his story was legit.

As we jogged, I looked over at Val, in her nondescript black shorts and plain wordless grey t-shirt. I could see she wasn't wearing a bra; she was almost as flat as I was.

"Do you ever think about, or want to, transition?" I asked.

"You mean become a guy? Because I'm so butch, ha!" Val laughed a genuine, hearty laugh.

"Well, yeah," I admitted.

"Honestly, no. The truth is, I don't really think about my own body when I desire girls, because all I feel is the desire, I just kind of forget about my body in a way that makes me indifferent to my breasts or vagina or ovaries or whatever. And I like that feeling because it took me a long time to like myself, the way I looked, and I think that's an achievement of sorts that I don't want to give up just so I can have a beard or chest hair or whatever. But that's just me."

"I can't imagine your having to work hard to feel good about yourself."

"You know, standards of beauty and sexiness are always changing. I've found that in terms of body self-esteem, all you can do is just hold 'em until you can bluff everyone else out. Before you know it, your pair of sixes don't look so bad! I'm sure you felt this too, though. I was born to be skinny and small-breasted, and in middle and high school, that wasn't the great way for a girl to look, even if she is a tomboy. It's weird to get called out as both a dyke and an ugly chick at the same time! I didn't really care but you get enough verbal violence heaped on you and even if you don't care, it hurts. But then I started modeling and then it was a whole other story, where being flat-chested and thin was a good thing, although I had to be someone else entirely—makeup, dresses, heels. Thank god the '80s were over by then and they at least let me keep my hair short. But if you told me when I was 13 that high fashion and butch lesbianism have something in common, I wouldn't have believed you. But don't get me wrong: I can't speak for butches who have big hips or breasts. Obviously there are plenty of butches who have big hips and big breasts who are totally fine with their bodies and their sense of masculinity has nothing to do with a female physique."

Just then, we were passed by a male jogger; he definitely wasn't running, but by this time Val and I were walking along with Delilah so he passed us easily on the slightly more inclined block. The male jogger moved quickly enough that I didn't see his face. From the back, I saw that he had kind of longish hair that didn't quite hit his shoulders flowing out of one of those tightly fitting caps that serious bicyclists wear. He looked quite fit, with strong sinewy muscles, V-shaped torso, a nice round booty-butt packed into short blue shorts, carved delts emerging out from a white perforated racer-back style nylon tank top, strong long arms swinging along with bulging calves. But he looked so stupid, with that tall beautiful body, jogging at the pace of a grandma, shoulders slumped in exhaustion and wrists breaking, flat-footed stride whacking his knees into a sad, pathetic form. And on his hat he had attached some kind of plastic device that reminded me of a beer guzzler, on which was affixed a headlight that was obnoxiously and dumbly shining up his route forward.

TOO MANY WELL TEQUILA SHOTS WITH NEITHER LEMON nor salt leading to projectile vomiting on the pool table, heaping florid verbal abuse upon an old man bartender who dared to card me but not the white, teen-looking frat boys next to me, screaming at another male bartender who kept serving everyone but my freckled, dissembling small town boyish lesbian compatriot: I've been eighty-sixed from a good half the bars in the Castro, which is funny because I've never been thrown out of a single bar South of Market, even though I've blacked out there more times and more often.

Sunday night, around ten, Tish and I were squeezed into the small, old leather-and-bear bar on Castro Street. In point of fact, it was the bar where I puked on the pool table. Luckily, bars in the Castro were packed enough often enough, and its bartenders without much memory—either by age or grace of character—that being eighty-sixed was never a permanent status. We were pummeled with man-fat, B.O. mixed with expensive colognes (orange, fennel, Szechuan peppercorn), and obnoxious disco music. Usually obnoxious disco music doesn't bother me at all, but maybe I wasn't drunk in the right way. So it was a relief when the Bee Gees play that funky music white boy I love the nightlife shit segued into a relatively recent song; from the opening bars I recognized it as a minor hit by an R&B girl group from DC. I was into this group enough to have bought both their two CDs because the lead singer seemed, incongruously, to be a closeted butch dyke; incongruous because the group's vocals were high-pitched, plaintive, pleading, even, as aggressive basslines and unforgiving, forthright lyrics spiked around them. This song that was playing at the bar, though, was really about pleading, and the sound of chimes, delicate and metallic, was a wash of thin knives mixed with sassy rhythmic blowing of plastic whistles. Together they all unrolled a red carpet for oncoming sweet vocals dressed in lyrics celebrating toxic codependency. Discovering comfort, I began swaying hard and enthusiastically to the song as the bartender set up my second Stoli and soda. Tish was barely a few sips into her first drink, a shit-thick Shiraz in a wine glass the size of a Big Gulp. But her drink was more an accessory befitting her environs.

We were sitting at the bar near the front whose glass window-wall opened into the sidewalk and made the area off the entrance a makeshift patio; there, you could hang practically half your body onto pedestrians. You could barely call it sitting; it was so crowded, the backless barstools crammed seat-to-seat, it was impossible to get up without having almost the entire bar get up then fall domino-style, to give you room to stand up and get up. So we were stuck, kind of perched on the uncomfortably brass-studded rim of the cheap red vinyl crackling into decades-hardened yellow foam, balancing our flesh against gravity with just tailbone and toe. It was also impossible to turn to see who was directly next to you. I didn't know who was next to me on the right side but to the left, I could see a few seats next to Tish an older gentleman in a fawn-colored three-piece suit in needle-thin corduroy, seemingly drinking alone. He was nursing, in a pace as elegant as his aura, a pint of dark beer. His face was age-spotted and dark with that tell-tale tan of the Caucasian-Californian, smooth but for very deep lines around his eyes, made deeper because he was smiling to himself. I wondered if he was happily getting fucked up—I hoped so. He was rather handsome, with a thick grey mustache matching a full head of grey hair cut in a way that made him look roguish and younger than his age, which was probably sixty. He might have looked even younger, but his light oxford shirt was collared by a wide, dark silk necktie patterned with pale, iridescent blue flowers that looked doubtlessly out of the '70s.

Tish, as always, looked fashionable—nothing on her ever looked nostalgic or backward. She was wearing comfortably-faded blue jeans that weren't skintight, rolled up over her ankles and bare feet in low-heeled sandals with lattices of very thin strips of tan leather held together with cunning little silver buckles. She also wore a fancy, loose-fitting summer sweater striped in Rasta colors. Her gently lightened and relaxed hair was loose and brushed totally off her face, and the fragile, delicately trimmed ends fell casually over her shoulders. Tish didn't carry a purse, and she never did. I've known femme dykes who carry purses as big as a suitcase, crammed with make-up and books and electronic devices and wallets the size of handbags and even bottles of gluten-free hot sauce. Some femmes hauled these monsters on their shoulders for hours at a time, even a whole evening, demonstrating simultaneously their bodily strength and feminine frivolity. Then there are femmes who carry perfectly proportioned purses just big enough to encase a wallet and cigarettes, maybe a cell phone. I suppose straight women carry purses in similar ways—I really don't know, everything I know about women I learned from lesbians. Tish held everything in the pocket of her jeans: a very tiny cell phone and a very expensive silver money clip for neat wads of cash and a credit card. I admired her minimalism as my own lazy wallet bulged with very little cash and a ton of plastic that all bore the name "Howie Song": driver's license, pass card-ID for work, Kaiser Permanente card, CVS membership card, BevMo! membership card, and credit cards that really all ought to have been cut up. Tish pulled a tenner from her clip and paid for my drink.

"But you're still on your first drink," I protested feebly and smilingly.

"Payment for services rendered," Tish joked. It was she who asked me to meet her here, unexpectedly depressed as she had become. She had had a dinner date with her most recent ex-girlfriend at a fancy French restaurant around the corner from the bar, in the hopes for a reconciliation that didn't end up happening.

"Now why did I even agree to meet her? She dumped me for that young chick, that straight girl from her class. I should have known better."

"Because you still have feelings for her, obviously," I said. "Otherwise, why do you still talk to her like every week?"

"You know that's just a lesbian thing; we never truly cut the line. Besides, with Deane, it's really her sister that I'm friends with. So when I talk to Melanie, it's hard to avoid Deane as a topic of conversation."

"Yeah, but it's different when Deane calls to check up on you every Thursday night. And chiding you if you don't open up enough for her."

Tish nodded tragically and laughed at herself.

Then a voice cut loud through the music and smells: "There are *so* many women in here tonight!"

It was most definitely a complaint, and it came from somewhere behind me. Both Tish and I snapped to attention and looked up and tried—in vain, of course, we couldn't really move—to look around and locate the bodily source of the voice. We couldn't figure out who had actually shouted.

"Interesting how one woman is 'so many women,'" Tish said in a loud but serene voice.

No one acknowledged her comment, but then, no one acknowledged the bitchy sexist complainant either.

"I suppose I am used to the casual misogyny of gay male culture and gay men, especially in San Francisco, but it's always a little disappointing when I'm faced with it," Tish said to me, her volume re-set towards me only.

"I know, me too. Like, that comment felt directed at me as well, somehow, maybe because I'm with you," I replied.

"Yes, but maybe the asshole sexist is a really nuanced reader of people—he's a fag after all living in a cruelly heterosexual world, even if he is sexist. He probably sensed that you are different from him, and everyone else in this bar."

It was true that I wasn't wearing black leather and metal rings, nor did I have a big hairy back and shoulders and wildly sculpted and carved facial hair. I was wearing an old black t-shirt bearing a cartoon caricature of the winking face of a lesbian folk singer who was quite popular in the late 1980s, with the insignia of the record company (a beautiful, almost cubist rendering of the Roman god Mercury) printed on the left sleeve like a military badge, and old, faded black jeans gone grey. But the jeans were blasted out at the butt to show my pink and black zebra-striped silk boxer shorts, so that, at least, felt a little more thematic.

"If I were here tonight cruising by myself, without you, would I be the token 'woman'?" I asked.

"Like I'm the token black lesbian at the Lex?" It was a serious question, but asked with a twinkle of nonchalance.

"But you don't really feel like a token black girl, do you?"

"No, I suppose not. I'm old enough to know full well the company I choose to keep. But sometimes it's a redux of my teenage years growing up in the Midwest. Barely any black kids at my high school, and among them, it felt as though my gayness, as suppressed as it was, created a kind of forcefield around me. It was tough being a young black girl, who desired girls, and looking like a geek I was, complete with big square thick glasses. Definitely hanging out with the other geeks I was the token black girl. The other day, Fei Fei was saying how having grown up in the Bay Area, she hadn't known there was such a thing as autumn. When she was a kid she hadn't known leaves on trees could turn red and yellow. I told her how beautiful certain trees could look in October in Iowa, when the branches go all silvery grey, a beautiful optical illusion of moss and fungus and dead bark mixing in with the new, and the leaves so yellow against the bright blue sky that it's not even gold; it's a different kind of flower blooming, leaves turning to daffodil or yellow daisy, or the sun itself. She just looked at me and looked and me and nodded but it was clear she was expecting me to say something about being black in the Midwest, not about the red oak trees whose leaves turn sunny in autumn."

I nodded, dumbly too, and then, feeling a little awkward, chose to catch instead the bartender's eye. I was transferring my nodding to him and pointing at my empty glass, mouthing "Another please" when I felt hard three taps on my shoulder. I twisted round, managing about 50 degrees.

"Yes?" I asked. Out of the obscured view of my shoulder I saw an angry-looking male face.

"Could you please turn around and face me for a

minute?" His stress on "please" was definitely anger rather than politesse.

"I really can't unless you get up. Can't you see there's no room?" I turned back to Tish with a sigh. I heard a minor tussle behind me and then the guy tapped me three hard times again. Somehow, he had made room to get up and push his own stool back away from the bar where he now stood, giving me room to get up and face him, which I did. As I stood facing the angry guy, I saw over his head, in a private little huddle near the back of the bar, Jeb. His straw-gold hair laying in crazy angles, those narrow wide nostrils, big stupid grin, flirtatiously surrounded by silver bears. But it couldn't be Jeb—Jeb wasn't totally gay, and as little as I knew him, I knew him well enough to know he wouldn't be caught dead wearing anything but solid colors in organic cotton—never that cheap red plaid flannel.

Away from what I hoped was a delusion, mirage, or hallucination, I turned back to the angry guy, who was looking me up and down. He was not wanting to pick me up. I too looked him up and down: he was around my age, and about three times my weight and a head shorter. I couldn't tell if he was muscular or chubby; I suspected a bit of both. He was wearing black leather pants, very tight, with, inexplicably, a pair of leather chaps over that. The chaps were a different color—red with yellow tuxedo stripes down the side. He wore black leather bracelets with metal loops hanging off them, and a similarly designed black leather harness with buckles and hoops, worn over a black t-shirt with a print of

Bettie Page bound and gagged and corseted and stilettoed. He had a lot of springy black hair all over his arms. His head hair was cut into a tidy mohawk. Small metal spheres and spikes sprung out of his septum, lip, ear lobes and even nasal bone. I was hit with the same feeling I got when, years ago, I stood but a few steps to a deer in the wild. She looked at me with a calm curiosity that was ever so slightly wary, and I could see her wet, black nose dilate and close in the rhythm of that feeling. She stood, beautiful as a picture; when I stepped, cautiously, even closer to her, I felt apprehensive and frightened. There was nothing in her smoothly bristled body and elegant limbs, her big black eyes, to be scared of, yet I was. The deer ran off, her white tail fluffy and shockingly huge.

"That cunt is a fucking homophobe," the guy hissed angrily to me.

I exchanged astonished looks with Tish. Turning back to the angry guy, I said, "What the fuck? Are you fucking crazy to talk about my friend like that?"

Obviously I was about to say more, but the guy interrupted me, his already quite high voice rising and sharpening to a point.

"I'm not talking about your friend. I'm talking about her." He stuck a heavily-ringed index finger into my sternum, pointing, again, three hard times. I was getting irritated.

"Her? Me?"

"Her," he said, pointing again to my chest. Finally I realized he was pointing not to me but to the lesbian folk singer whose face was on my shirt. I couldn't think of anything to say. Was this lesbian folk singer a homophobe? I didn't understand.

The angry guy's words were now spitting at me. "Are you a total fucking ignoramus?"

My irritation had melted into genuine confusion. "But she's just a folk singer, and a lesbian besides," I protested.

"No. She's come out and said she was confused and found God and heterosexuality and that gay people deserve to burn in Hell. What's your problem?"

"Hey, man, what is your problem? It's just a t-shirt." Tish now joined in, but the angry guy ignored her.

I noticed that my third round of Stoli had materialized in all the fuss, and I was tempted to throw it in the guy's face but I wasn't that drunk yet—and also I wanted to drink my drink. So instead, I said: "Fuck off you fat queen, and take your sad, nasty-ass piercings with you."

The angry guy's friends emerged from behind him and took individual, lit shapes out of the shadows forming a formidable fort around their friend. This is why I couldn't see if the angry guy's face had fallen to my violence, or, remained righteously angry. At the same time, I felt a strong hand grip my shoulder from across the bar.

"You need to leave. Your friend also." It was the bartender.

"You fucking kidding? He harassed me first!" I said in hysterical but earnest protest.

The bartender shook his head solemnly. "I'm not going to ask you twice. You need to leave. Tom!" He stood on his tip toes and yelled and motioned to the bouncer slacked at the entrance.

"Alright. We're going, don't get your lace panties in a knot. It's truly sad you have to get your big strong boyfriend involved, a big grown man like you," I said, doing my best Angie Dickinson.

"Out," said the bartender.

I took the third Stoli and soda and gulped it down in one go. As I took Tish's arm and we walked out, I caught the eye of the handsome old gentleman in his fawn suit. He was no longer smiling but he met my eyes with a sadness that creased his eye-lines even more. His beer was only half empty, and sat plaintively next to his resting watched wrist, warming. I wondered if it really was Jeb I saw at the back of the bar, playing the young otter.

We poured out of the bar puffing righteousness and resigned laughter. We walked a bit on Castro Street and then 18th before turning to the side street where Tish had parked. You would expect a lawyer to drive a Benz or at least a Lexus, but in fact, Tish didn't own a car for her first many years in San Francisco, and now drove an inexplicably big Easter egg-blue Ford van from the '80s. It was wedged elegantly and magically between two guppie vehicles with barely four fingers' width bumper to bumper. I didn't tell Tish about seeing maybe-Jeb at the bar when I asked to use her cell phone to call him. She pulled the cell phone out and handed it to me. It was iridescent green, the color of a Green Apple Jolly Rancher and the size of one of those Snickers bars made for handing out to kids on Halloween. I punched in Jeb's cell phone number. When he finally answered I stopped my breath to listen hard, to see if I could hear crowd noise, drink glasses and beer bottles scuttling, perhaps the indignation of the pierced leather queen.

"Hello. Who is this?" Jeb's voice was dry and icy, a tone I hadn't heard before. But then—I'd never really had the chance to hear him talk to anyone but me and Delilah, the way things were between us. The backdrop to his voice was all fuzzed out; I couldn't situate the sonic blur.

"Jeb, it's Howie."

"Oh, hey. What are you up to?" He dropped his guard quickly and sounded more relaxed.

"I'm calling from a friend's cell phone. We just had drinks in the Castro. What are you doing?"

"I'm just getting off work. Why, what's up?"

I wondered if he was telling the truth. It's true that the restaurant stayed open late on the weekends for its popular bar, but I doubted that Jeb would have had to stick around to cook the dinner menu during what was most likely cocktail hours. Still, I didn't press it.

"Do you feel like hanging out?" I ventured.

"In the Castro?"

"Well yeah, why not? I'm still up for another drink. You could get here pretty fast from the Civic Center on the F line."

There was a pause, a long one. Finally, Jeb said: "I'm really tired, Howie. I've been at work since 10 a.m. because I was filling in brunch duty for a co-worker who has the flu."

I paused too, though mine not as long as his. "Would you be up for hanging out at my house? Obviously you're really close. You might have to wait a little bit though, my friend is giving me a ride back."

"Yeah, that sounds cool."

I was gratified that he didn't hesitate. I handed the phone back to Tish, and asked her if she had known this thing about the folk singer. She answered: "No, not at all. It's pretty disappointing, though, even if I've never been a big fan of her music."

"I guess I can't wear this shirt any more. It sucks because I really like this shirt. I've had it ever since high school. That guy couldn't know that it was probably the first piece of gay memorabilia I ever got."

"No, he couldn't, but probably he ought to have guessed. In the end, you two are probably the same babes in the same mean old woods." She turned the key in the ignition and the Ford rumbled eagerly, if slowly, to life. Tish began a series of micromovements, delicate turns back and forth upon the steering wheel punctuated by gear shifts, to get the wheels of the van to angle precisely in position to be able to pull out of the tight parking space without a scratch to any of the three cars involved.

As she made the final turn of the steering wheel, she said ponderously: "You could wear the t-shirt ironically. It's not like she was a homophobe when that album came out. It could be an homage to her lesbian history, an act of mourning and melancholia."

"That's good enough for me," I said eagerly, and we tore down through Noe as fast as the old van could, then joined the indolent traffic onto Market Street.

Jeb was already on my stoop when we pulled up to my

house. His bicycle was nowhere to be seen. He was just sitting there, legs akimbo, feet unhinged from ankles, elbow on knee and chin on palm, cigarette burning away between oblivious fingertips, not pretending to be doing anything cooler than waiting for me.

"Little Orphan Annie," Tish said with a wink and a kiss, and I got out to go to him.

I didn't tell him anything about the deer-leather queen or the little black girl in Iowa. We just walked together into my place as always, and while we stripped Jeb gave Delilah a big pet and allowed her to slurp his naked ankle and I gave her a big old oily bully stick. She carried it into the bathroom and lay on the bathmat, which was a rug made entirely of grey and black rags. She flopped down on her stomach and went to work on the bully stick, obediently bored. In the meantime, Jeb and I finished getting naked and between kisses I went and poured us the usual mugs of booze—tonight, half a bottle of Evan Williams.

We drank, made out, jerked each other, and eventually positioned ourselves on the edge of my bed in readiness of my riding his cock. He sat holding and balancing me straddled over his big strong thighs that were soft as clouds. My butt cheeks were spread and stretched between the tops of his knees. Jeb kissed me long, hard, and passionately. Unlike most people, who keep their mouth closed until the very moment it touched that of another, Jeb opened his mouth from the moment he started leaning toward me. If they had made a video of us kissing, shot in profile, they would see that his mouth was open, tongue almost hanging out while we were a good two inches apart. Between kissing he deftly held me at a purposeful distance—holding me by the waist but just far enough for him to kiss and suck and finger my tits as if to encourage them to grow into breast-tips. This was, I imagined, the way he would kiss a woman before he pressed her warm cunt onto him. This thought made me hot, but also something else. I thought about how we'd always fucked in my bed, never anywhere else, not even in the big, bedroom-sized single-toilet wheelchair-accessible restroom in the restaurant where he worked, even when I met him during his lunch break; and certainly, never his apartment, never his bed. I knew he didn't live too far, he lived in the Tenderloin, near the Lumiere cinema on Sacramento Street. But he never told me even the cross street, and he made his withholding feel like the casual thoughtlessness of the innocent, of innocent friendship. I wondered if he was one of those people whose jobs were authentically unalienated labor. I wondered if his kitchen was a more modest, aspirational version of the big spaceship kitchen for which he donned his white coat and received his not ungenerous paycheck. I wondered if his refrigerator and stove fixture were that same professional steampunk chrome—unlikely if he rented his apartment, but one never knows—and I concluded that it wasn't, as he most likely rented, but I was sure he made sure to rent a place that had a gas stove rather than plebeian electric coils. I was most certain he owned sets and subsets of gleaming steel knives: miniature samurai swords. He wouldn't care so much about plates or flatware but he'd care about knives. And drinkware: lead-free crystal goblets and teensy cups for shots and aperitif. Or was it me that cared about knives that could cut glass and wine crystal as carved as chandeliers?

As we kissed and he rolled my tits in his fingertips, Jeb whispered hoarsely, "I'm really hard and drippy. Sit on my cock now."

I began adjusting my hips to obey, but for some reason I said, impulsively: "Actually, I would like to fuck you."

Jeb looked at me with refocused narrow pupils, but the look had no surprise in it. His face settled into pacific serenity, a serene bemusement. Without a word, he let go of me and scooched back on his elbow and drew his legs up.

It's hard to maneuver and fuck a person bigger than you, and I'm pretty sure Jeb had a good 50 pounds on me. I could see his asshole, the puffy, ripe pucker. Not more than a few weeks ago, my general practitioner told me I should try not to bear down when I sat on the toilet—it would exacerbate my bright red hemorrhage. Yet here was Jeb, bearing down and across for the promise of my swollen cock-tip. I spat on my hand and lubed it. A rank smell, not unpleasant, rose up around us. I spat again onto my palm and massaged his hole, which was surprisingly hairless, spongy and smooth. His tailbone was a smooth round paleolithic nub. Jeb made some guttural sounds of pleasure-surprise. I rolled the condom meant for him onto my own hard cock and put the tip of the whole rubberized thing against his asshole. I pushed in without warning and his guttural sound turned into a grunt of pain. I didn't ask him if this was OK, if he was OK; I was not going to baby him. He had enough of my spit in there and since, I guessed, he did not douche in preparation for me, he also had enough semi-liquefied cells down there to ease the pain of his receptivity. As I pushed in with one hard thrust, he yelped once in pain but then bit down on his lip. His asshole stretched willingly and he stretched his neck back, long and incongruously swan-like, and vibrated. Once inside I fucked him slowly, and to my gratitude, he lifted his legs up and moved his whole southern half of his body closer to my forward strokes inward. He was quite strong, so at some point he used his arms to hold his legs up so while I fucked him, my hands could be free. I noticed for the first time that Jeb was kind of soft. He wasn't chubby, he definitely had big muscles, but he was rounded all over: his delts, biceps, were all round and cuddly as velvet balloons, and so too were the beginning of the love handles at his waist. I had never known his butt was so big, either. I squeezed the fleshy cheeks as I pushed my cock into him and they felt warm and beautiful, not like the steroidal stones I felt on most of the guys I've fucked. He began moaning in a different register; the initial intensity flattened into a satiated hum. "Oh baby," he moaned, before the words dissolved into just gloating in the pleasure. Then I put my arms down towards his chest and cupping his ribs with my hands, I played with his little hard scarlet nipples with my thumbs, moving them back and forth over them and the errant hairs around them like a video game console. When I was close, I pulled out, again without warning and came on his pubic area. He reached around and smushed my sperm all around himself, including around his anus. I noticed then that he had already come all over his belly, his own jizz pooling in his innie navel. I fell forward a bit and let our cocks press against each other and against his belly, underside of cock to underside of cock, and I continued to hump him in a slurpy, lackadaisical way. By now my balls, which had hardened and jumped into the hollows of my thighs, had re-softened and hung back down peacefully. We dry-humped, letting our testicles press and pull apart stickily against each other, and we both felt a good, spongy feeling like bread dough and Nerf balls.

"Have you ever been fucked before?" I asked Jeb as I picked at with the weird little patch of hair nestled in his muscly cleavage.

Jeb answered my question with typical and continuous serenity: "Not by a guy, no. I do live in San Francisco, so I do have sex toys. I have a vibrating butt-plug."

I pictured Jeb's fat pale butt holding a black rubber-coated bean-electrode. I saw the butt-plug as an ancient Egyptian scarab, obviously purloined by the British, insect-black and arcane in its obsidian shine, poking out playfully and mystically from his obscured asshole, disgusting as a magnified blue black tick. I wanted to ask Jeb if he was truly bisexual or if he was an intense cock-tease or if he had become gay because of me. Instead, I said: "Is my cock inside you better than a buxom chick pushing the on-switch on your vibrator?"

As soon as I uttered the words, as usual, I regretted them. The fact is, I'd been worried that I was some kind of transitional object for Jeb, and I know from experience: a bisexual guy fucks me, and regularly, with strategically timed words of romance or at least affection, and then dumps me, not for a woman whom he was used to, but for a man, a man more manly than I. Was I some kind of androgynous, femme creature that the guy used to get used to his own homosexuality? But no: I knew myself to be, not without some disappointment, that I was after all, nothing but a male human being.

Jeb adjusted his body and with the pad of his left thumb, traced an abstract but clear path from my collarbone to my sternum, where the lateral edges of my rib bones stretched away from my pectoral muscles into the skin covering them.

"I love you for your clavicle and these little bones right here," he said.

I wanted to ask him what he meant; instead I bit my tongue and licked him all over. It was the first and only time Jeb said "I love you" to me, but also technically he never said "I love you" because to me he never said those three words as a single sentence, full-stop.

OoO

FIRST: I'M STANDING STILL AND UPRIGHT, ARMS FALLING *straight down, palms turned inward without touching the upper part of my thighs, but my fingers still slightly curved; legs flexed straight with feet slightly apart, turned out between a duck and a soldier; chin up, but not so much that I look like an asshole or you can see up my nostrils; neck lengthened but relaxed; shoulders back but not so much that I look like a '50s showgirl; my stomach relaxed—no need to suck my gut in—but holding just enough tension below my navel as it links up to my vertebrae, my usual Chi breathing machine; perfectly straight vertebrae holding up a back that is curved just gently enough to emphasize the brandy-snifter curve of my butt. I'm making my muscles hold pairs of paradoxes like alternating beads on a hippie love-bead necklace, also known as my best ballet posture.*

I got talked into doing this nude modeling thing by one of the assistant directors of the company. Mike was a Latino gay guy in his early forties who was sort of in the middle of the institutional hierarchy of the company, and on the way up, so I figured it wouldn't hurt to play ball with him, although I usually hate playing ball. Besides, he was one of those administrators who feel they have a special kinship with artists—he used to be a painter himself—the kind who is always sweet and says your name multiple times while telling you that the company has had to switch insurance companies so your shrink is no longer in network or you have to switch to an even more generic kind of meds. Really, though, that kind of sweetness is necessary in his line of work. So when he told me that he was putting together a "salon" (his word) and he needed an "artist's model" (again, his words) and that he would really like me to be that model, I didn't think too hard, even though I was only getting paid a couple hundred dollars for an event that was charging a minimum donation of $1000 per head, maybe because I thought Mike was a handsome guy, maybe because I thought he had always liked me, maybe because he could introduce me to some nice gay guys if he didn't like me romantically or sexually, but probably not because I was ambitious.

The salon was to benefit the summer youth program offering free dance classes—not just ballet but tap and modern and even hip hop—for at-risk and low-income youth. In the five years I've been with the company, I've never taken part in this program, not because I don't believe in helping at-risk and low-income kids but because I don't like children too much. So I'm not sure why I got singled out to do this since there were certainly guys with better faces and bodies than me. Maybe word got around to him that I'm a slut or at least, that I'm very happy without any clothes on. In any case, this salon was an evening of rich people getting to drink a lot of expensive and exclusive California wine and draw a nude model under Mike's flattering but artistically knowledgeable and enlightening tutelage.

I was just ready to take my clothes off when Mike handed me a Syrah-colored silk dressing gown and said: "Wear this when you enter. You'll go to a platform in the middle of the room, and when you step onto it, stand dressed just for a few seconds. Don't acknowledge anyone in the room, no eye contact, no nodding or anything like that. Just stare straight ahead. Then just drop your robe. The whole event will be a little over an hour, and you'll do six poses for about ten minutes each, give or take a minute. I'll be walking around so when it's time to switch poses, I'll just call it out. Be free, do what you feel, you'll be great and beautiful. There's a chair and a block there for you. Just one thing though: your first pose has to be just standing stock still."

Second: I'm sitting on the chair. I plant my ass in the middle of the seat and make my legs parallel with the legs of the chair, which means they are spread quite far apart. I lift my right foot and reaching down, holding my right ankle with both hands—right hand cupping over and left just slightly supporting it, fingers splayed a bit—I bring the foot up to my left thigh, right above the kneecap, and let it rest there. I keep my hands as they were around the right ankle. I bend both elbows and bring my chest towards this thing I've created with my right ankle and my left thigh, which breaks my elbows into a pair of wing-like, sharply pointed parentheses, the right elbow now resting slightly on the inside of my right thigh. My chest gets concave; I drop my head.

The first thing I remember about meeting Scott, my ex, was the chair to which he tied my left wrist—or rather, the leg of the chair to which he tied my left wrist. Of course this isn't entirely accurate; I had met Scott before he tied me down. He was the host of the party, a friend of an old fuck buddy named Ramy, and obviously I had to have seen his face between the time I passed through his door and when I got naked on all fours. But it's like memories of being a child: supposedly you ought to remember the face or nipple of your mother before you remember that nubby yellow stuffed bunny but when someone asks you what your first memory is, you say: "A nubby yellow stuffed bunny."

So it was with Scott, Scott Tierney. I knew his last name that day because as a part of the safety procedure, the four guys who were tops had to show me their ID cards before depositing them in the key bowl on the narrow table over the shoes, next to the front door. Still, my first memory of Scott is the chair leg: a thin round dowel of polished wood the width of a fishing pole, that came to a soft round nub upon the floor. It seemed unrealistic that such thin legs could support the grey stuffed leather armchair seat, but they did. Totally naked, on my knees and elbows, I took the place of the low coffee table that had been pushed out of the way against a far wall. Scott was dressed, I don't remember exactly what he was wearing—probably a white t-shirt and pants. He pulled the soft leather armchair towards my left side and unspooled white nylon rope to tie my left wrist to the chair leg. He left about five inches of give between the chair leg and my wrist, and while he knotted the rope to the chair leg very tight and immoveable, he made the knot on my left wrist—as he did the ones on my right wrist and both my ankles—secure, but took care not to press the tight knot against my skin. This was due to my caveat:

"I'm a dancer and I can't injure my legs," I had told him, which he remembered.

Four chairs were placed like four trees being planted in a re-arbor forest, the boundaries of which were my four limbs. My right wrist was tied to a white powder-coated metal kitchen chair, and another one anchored my right ankle. My left ankle was tied to a heavy kind of stool or ottoman with a thick pink tapestry cover. For about an hour, Scott, Ramy and two other guys whose names I can't remember fucked me through my asshole and mouth. The safe word was "Dusty." No one could strike me with their hand or feet in any way, although I agreed that if my teeth grazed a cock, the owner of the cock could lightly slap me and say something to the effect of, "Suck better, you little dickbitch," which did happen a couple times.

As these things go, all five of us became totally abstracted over the hour. I couldn't tell you who was in my mouth even though they were sitting in that soft leather armchair right in front of me; it might have been the tears streaming down my face. Of course, I couldn't tell at all who was fucking me from behind because I was tied to the four trees which made it impossible for me to crane my head back. I felt the brush of pubic hair chafing my asshole and the thud of cum-heavy balls bouncing against my spread butt cheeks, which over time felt like wrecking balls moving in a comforting rhythm of a metronome, with me the piano eking out Schubert dances. Occasionally I heard the snap of condoms being taken off before semen sprayed over my backside, or else simply dropped on the floor as they had jizzed inside me. No condoms were required to fuck my mouth, and if the tops became bodiless, I just became a pencil drawing with lines made in little points of pain. Once, in a gallery in Los Angeles, at a show for a famous female artist, I saw a huge painting that took up an entire wall that was actually just a bare white canvas with a crude line drawing of a woman (person?) with their legs spread, fingers digging into her vagina. But the lines were so crude that the person had no face, their hair just a black scratch and their fingers were barely lines. But the drawing moved me tremendously, and it's exactly how I felt as cum was being dumped into my butt and mouth. The guys who weren't inside me wandered in and out of the room. Sometimes they sat on one of the free chairs and watched and stroked their limp dicks back to an erection. One of them took a little nap against one wall. My own cock was hard as a rock and dripping with precum, my balls too were heavy and full of cum. As my knees and elbows became rubbed red against the smooth floor, my cock and balls swung back and forth with ominous weight. No one was allowed to touch my genitals; I was not allowed to come. Still, some hands reached under and teased my hard purple balls as they fucked me.

The last guy in my mouth was Scott. He was leaning back so far in the armchair that he was nearly laying down, with his t-shirt hiked up so he could play lightly with his nipples that were very hard, very pointy, nearly red under a cover of long black hair that covered his chest and stomach with a flat electric static. As he teased his nipple with the flat of one palm, he reached down with his free hand and held my jaw. He told me to suck harder. I did, and he came, and the sperm I sucked into my throat was just little droplets; all that was left in his balls. He patted my cheek lightly and said, "I think that's about it."

I flopped down into the wood floor and lay there, my hard cock and heavy balls pulsing uncomfortably against myself. I stayed there while everyone left, still tied up. Scott too went out of the room but eventually came back, fully dressed, and untied me very slowly, as if he were trying to drain every last second of the whole experience.

"You were great," he said. "Are you OK? Do you want some water? Or beer? Or I can make some tea?"

I just shook my head, my mouth gummed up with dried sperm, my butthole like a neon circle. Suddenly, Scott kneeled down beside me and took me into his arms. He picked me up and carried me into the bathroom, where he began running water into the bathtub. As we waited for the tub to fill, he made me sit up next to it, on the impossibly plush bathmat, and gave me a tall glass of water, which he made me drink; he held me until the tub was full and put me in. The water was perfectly warm—steam rising, but not at all scalding. As I sat there, the little pains dissipated from my body and my skin began to feel like skin. He washed me gently with a pale soap that smelled of lemon and chamomile. We didn't speak.

After he dried me with a towel, he carried me into his bedroom and put me down next to his bed. He pulled back the covers and told me to get in, which I did. I lay there, my head resting on the fluffy pillow, my back drinking up the soft cotton of the sheets, and watched Scott take off his clothes. It was then that I saw how handsome he was. He had four dimples on his face—one on his chin, another on his right cheek and two right next to one another on his left cheek. I guess he was what you'd call "Black Irish": long, upward sloping eyes that looked almost Asian, blue irises, long black lashes, pale creamy skin, thick wavy hair that was truly black. I saw that his entire body was covered with this same black hair, but the body hair was quite thin, long and straight, and lay flat against his skin. Even his pubic hair was weirdly straight. I saw he was hard again. So was I.

He lay down next to me and began to touch my cock and massage my balls. I looked down and saw that my balls were still so full of cum that it was dark with the blood filling all the dilated veins beneath the skin. My balls looked like two small plums, hard and unripe, and just as heavy. Scott handled them with the gentleness of a farmer assessing livestock. He opened the drawer of his bedside table and took out a tube of lube, and squirting some onto his hand, stroked my cock and massaged my balls. He then took his slippery hand and began working a finger into my asshole. I let out a little involuntary yelp.

"That hurts," I said.

Scott ignored me and put a second finger in. Again, it hurt, but I was harder than ever. My nipples had become tight red cones and Scott put one in his mouth and sucked softly as he repositioned my body a little to its side and pushed his hard cock into my asshole. He fucked me steadily, gently, insistently until I came all over myself. My balls hurt like hell and the tip of my penis felt like it was bleeding. But still—when Scott pulled out to finish himself off on his own belly, I felt keening disappointment, a yearning.

Third: the block is the cloudy color of driftwood, its whirls of grain so deeply grooved it looks tattooed. I move the chair off the round platform and replace it with the block. I stand at one end of the block, my body parallel to its long edge, and sit down on the edge of the short edge, my legs splayed out. I lower my upper body onto the block, and its long edge ends at the bottom of my scapula. For a moment I lay on the block , a very uncomfortable bed. I stretch out, my legs splayed straight out in front of me, my back arching as I let my head, shoulders and chest drop down. My neck crooks my head back and I can feel my hair touch the surface of the posing platform. I let my arms go akimbo. I spread my legs out, lift my bum just a little, and stretch my entire body lengthwise, letting the block do the work of giving the illusion that I am an arched table whose weight rests on the joints of my ten toes.

Two weeks earlier I asked some of my wealthier friends if they would want to donate a tax-deductible $1000 to drink special wine and draw me naked. Tish said yes. She was actually an art major in college, and I saw her near the center of the room, working her charcoal with a confident, self-knowing fury—brows furrowed and eyes concentrated studiously—behaving as if she had no idea who I was, and I was just a collection of black dust and white fiber. She is such a professional. Kala was in Los Angeles of course and couldn't come but she said that she would buy a ticket, and if someone wanted to go in her place, they were welcome. Each of the dozen or so easels that encircled me—all strangely polished to greasy slickness but also antique-looking old—had thumbtacked to its stand a heavy square card edged in fine dots of gilt, upon which bore the hand-calligraphed name of the guest. An empty easel on the edge of the second row of circles said: "Ms. Kala Young Kenney." I had asked Fei Fei, too, because after all, she owned her own business. But she didn't buy a ticket.

One week before, Wednesday night, Fei Fei and I were having drinks at the Lexington, at a table near the entrance. I was distracted to a trance, though, watching a couple playing pool. The taller woman, wearing a very dark purple lipstick and a banged ponytail like Gidget or Barbie, was obviously the skilled pool player teaching the other, shorter woman, shaved head like a young boy and clean pressed work pants and shirt, how to play. The shorter woman was scowling a lot, and clearly not enjoying not being very good at playing pool. She was expressing her displeasure through a languid, lackadaisical voice and attitude. Gidget/Barbie took no notice and continued pelting her partner with chipper instructions in a surprisingly husky voice, alternating with playful smooches. Her partner scowled some more at being smooched.

"I wonder why you asked me," Fei Fei suddenly said, breaking my trance. The mood of the evening seemed to change immediately.

"Asked you what?" I asked her.

"To this charity drawing thing."

"I thought it would be fun?"

"Did you ask anyone else? Or just me?"

"Well, I asked Kala and Tish, too."

Fei Fei looked at her Mezcal Margarita as if it had climbed up on her head and took a long piss. Finally, she shrugged and swiped the salt rim off her glass, and began flicking the crystals across the table. It felt as though she was flinging them at me.

"Why do you hold your wine glass like that?" she asked as she flicked, her eyes trained on the salt crystals.

"Like what?"

"Grabbing the bulb of the glass like it was a beer bottle or a soup bowl. You're supposed to hold a wine glass by the stem."

I was taken aback by the tone of her voice, which was not at all aggressive, but rather quietly instructive, and factual.

"What difference does it make? It's cheap white wine, and we're at the Lex."

"I guess you are trying to be good, drinking wine." She insinuated the word "wine" with an irony elegant beyond sarcasm.

"Yes, I'm trying to be good," I answered earnestly.

"Well, Howie, when you hold the wine glass incorrectly like that it makes you look like a barbarian."

"A *barbarian?*" I asked, flabbergasted.

"A *brute,*" she answered.

By this time our voices had become quite loud. The couple playing pool had gotten bored and left their game unfinished; they sat at the bar having beers in pint glasses and laughing softly together, occasionally looking over towards us. It didn't feel like an unkind laughter, but it was still a laughter. At least they seemed to be getting along better now.

The last time Fei Fei and I had a fight had been three years ago, when I told her I was moving in with Scott. We were at the Lex then, too, although sitting side by side at the bar. She didn't say anything nor look at me when I told her; she gave a nod of acknowledgement of facts and we moved onto different topics of conversation. But afterwards, she didn't call me or answer my calls for fourteen whole days, at the end of which I found a thick envelope wedged under my door. The envelope was blank, neither addressee nor addressor. Inside was a four-page handwritten letter from Fei Fei in which she listed all the reasons why she thought moving in with Scott into his place was a mistake, and what an essentially terrible and tyrannical person Scott was, and how deeply sad she was about our impending loss of friendship due to this decision of mine which was equivalent to self-mutilation, that unlike Scott she loved me through alcoholism and bulimia, how much she would miss me but that she still judged me, and loved me, and could never forgive me.

She wrote in a close, small, infinitely legible hand, on both sides of the paper. I was so angry with the thoughts and feelings she expressed in the letter that I refused to take her calls for the following fourteen days, during which I moved in with Scott. Sometime after that, Fei Fei and I ran into each other at Doc's Clock, got drunk and back together.

I downed the rest of my wine and sulked at the empty glass. The sun, almost setting, still coming in through the thick warped window above our heads and bouncing off the red walls of the bar, gave a coating of creamsicle-orange to my drink glass, Fei Fei, the wobbly endearing table between us, Delilah under us caught between short pink panting and sympathetic whimpering at the two human arguing voices, the jukebox with its doll's screens of CD booklets and that pinball machine beyond us sitting longside flush against the wall, so polite that when you play, others don't see the flashing lights and jumping balls, just hear the toy whirrs and sounds of knocking and breaking bone, of bright spring-loaded balls absorbed into the polite, subdued metal plates of its sides and uncertain legs.

"I had no idea you judged me like this," I said.

"I'm not judging you. I'm just telling you what I see and what others see when they look at you."

"That British imperialism in Hong Kong really rubbed off on you after all," I said. I tried to sound the words bitchily but they were strung together so awkwardly I was suddenly overwhelmed with embarrassment. I stood up with an equally awkward abruptness, and Delilah too got up and began whimpering at me for real, licking my hand. When I didn't respond she pattered over to Fei Fei and licked her hand, whimpering between licks.

"Oh, I'm sorry my lovely. It's OK sweetie," Fei Fei said to Delilah in a high, sweet, friendly, sing-song voice of a yuppie parent. The fact that she used this happy voice at this moment, even for Delilah who obviously has no part in this, made me irritated and pissed. I jerked Delilah away by her lead and went over and paid the bill, and left Fei Fei sitting still at our table. Delilah and I walked all the way home, but we stopped at the Kilowatt for a couple shots of bourbon, a beer and a bowl of clean cold water.

Fourth: pulling myself up into the sky, not just the ceiling, my arms and legs form one unbroken line; S/M torture hook in the clouds. Then shake the ropes loose, and I put my hands behind my head, push against the base of my skull and stretch in a way that bares the wild black bush of my armpits and arches my back into a C, italicized.

An old female voice, with the swing of many glasses of wine, barely audible above the general gentlefolk's din of the room: "I thought dancers were supposed to look like gods. This guy is positively scrawny."

Fifth: I pull the chair up back onto the platform. I stand in front of it, resting just the tender parts of my wrists on its back, which is unexpectedly high, so that the arms feel more uncomfortable than I anticipated, and the pull it forces in my delts and my spine makes my butt stick out. I bend my right knee and put it on the seat of the chair, turning that foot inward into a slight pointe. The wood of the chair is neither warm nor cold, and its ambivalent temperature feels kind of gross. I turn my head as far as it can to the left, my eyes downcast the whole time, and I watch the bone of my shoulder through my skin, the two light freckles.

That chair was quite devotional. The high back was empty of any horizontal slats, and the two framing vertical slats had strange jagged edges facing each other. As they joined at the top, the jags were replicated in little crown shapes at each end, but the middle was quite smooth and almost round. It was heavy as hell, even though from afar it looked quite delicate, spindly, even. But you didn't have to try to heft it to know that it was heavy; when you got up close you saw that the seat was quite thick, and the legs were very square and substantial. Running along the square edges were chipped, painted gilt lines. I don't know anything about wood but I thought about trees.

I got a splinter in my knee from that chair. I felt it shooting in but didn't see it until I got home that night: a thin red line with a speck of gold. I'm usually good at getting garbage out of my flesh, but I really should have slept on it. Instead, drunk with that expensive red wine from California, I took my sewing needle, ran it through the flame of my lighter and tried to dig the thing out. I think I actually pushed it further in. I'm not sure if I ever got the little piece of tree out of me. But I must have, because I didn't die of blood poisoning. Still, the area did stay injured for a while and now I have a little dot of new pink skin, a little three-dimensional oval that sometimes looks like a mole or pimple or blister, and this skin-bud, my tiny buddy, sometimes mocks me, sometimes deigns to decorate me. It would annoy me but I have a lot of scars on both my knees.

Sixth: I sprawl on the floor on my side and left elbow, as if with a paperback book in hand and dog curled into me.

After the last pose, I got up and put my borrowed silk dressing gown back on and took a half-hearted bow to the half-hearted patter of hands—fingertips on wrists, fingertips on palms, that sort of applause, which was fine with me. Mike came out and warbled some words of thanks to me and gushed to the generosity of the donors, which was I guess appropriate. He hadn't told me where to go so I began weaving in through the crowd of easels towards Tish, who gave me a big hug and put her arm around me in a nice squeeze.

Two boys came out wheeling a big linen-covered tack-board that took up an entire wall. Mike then invited all the donors to come forward and put up their drawings, and to "keep drinking all the fabulous wine." Tish handed me her glass, quite full and red.

"I'll get another. You look like you need this," she said, and she was right. I wonder if Tish could empathize with mutely being a body; after all, she was a lawyer who made her living by talking, and talking, I imagined from movies and television, in a forceful, elegant, emphatic voice. A waiter came around and offered Tish her choice of bubbly or Pinot Noir; she chose the Pinot and we matched.

I looked at the ten drawings she made of me. They were really quite beautiful: she had done them all in purple pencil, and they were surprisingly detailed and realistic. The lines were fine, and made me think of threads being pulled and loosed in rhythm to an ornate melody. The muscles seemed to be my muscles, the hair seemed to be my hair; the giant birthmark on the back of my left thigh seemed to be my own birthmark. Yet strangely, I couldn't recognize these drawings, skillfully drawn as old medical textbooks, as my own body, which incidentally had nothing to do with the fact that Tish had not drawn my face into any of them. Not that she left my face blank; she just had me turn my head away in every picture, as if my ear and hair and the diagonal of my neck muscle were my face.

"These are so good. I didn't know you could draw so well!" I said.

"Old skills. But I don't like to draw faces; they never seem to look right to me."

There's something to what Tish said. When we went up to the linen board to pin up a couple of Tish's drawings, I didn't recognize my body in anyone else's drawings, either. Some of them were horrible, but some were really very good. But none of them seemed to be me, and I don't think that feeling had anything to do with the fact that I went on to drink about a bottle and half worth of that expensive Cali Pinot Noir.

0o0

WHEN I LIVED WITH SCOTT, IN HIS HOUSE, HE WOULD make me suck his cock every morning, as soon as he woke up. I had to swallow his sperm every morning. We didn't live together very long, a few weeks shy of a year. Long before we moved in together I'd discovered that he liked morning fellatio, but since we didn't live together it didn't seem weird or a big deal to suck his cock when I was barely awake. At the end of the first week after I moved into his apartment, it still didn't seem weird or a big deal that I had sucked him to orgasm seven mornings in a row, because he made it seem like love-fueled lust for me: he would wake me up by wiggling his hard-on against the crack of my ass. His precum against my ass felt cozy, like a small heated pebble. Then he would reach around and play with my nipples, rolling them around with his fingertips, drawing them out until they reached the long, hard pointed shape that made both of us happy. My little red towers; no, *his* little red towers. He might suck on them for a bit before he kissed me on the mouth and then, as we got wrapped up in each other, he would gently push my head down to his crotch, where I would happily burrow my nose in his soft black pubes and suck him until he came. Then, I would go back to sleep and he would get up and put the coffee on.

But after a month or so, he dispensed with the love movements altogether. One day, I was shaken out of sleep by his hard cock slapping around my nose and mouth. I opened my eyes and saw that he had gotten out of the covers and climbed over my face. He didn't say anything, just pushed the tip of his cock against my lips until they parted and let him in. I sucked willingly because I was in love. And he would then let his fingers linger in my hair as I sucked; he would massage my scalp, or feel my earlobes, and sometimes, he'd gently plug my earholes with fingertips that fit perfectly, and all I could hear was the hum of my own greedy cocksucking. He fucked my mouth and kept his penis in until he made sure I swallowed every bit of his sperm, and then he got up to put the coffee on.

This was the new routine and still I didn't mind: he didn't have a long penis. The length of his cock, when erect, from shaft to tip, was exactly the distance between the opening of my mouth and the precipice of my throat. It was a short cock, but thick, with a weirdly pointy tip. He looked funny when he was naked because he was shorter than me and quite muscular, and he stood as if pulled by an invisible rig from above. He had the kind of body one doesn't see much these days: a very 1980s kind of fit body, in which the muscles were built up in a way that looked like two long triangles stacked tip to tip on top of each other. When he stood his small but thick penis would sprout out from his crotch, standing at attention. Even when he was soft his cock looked like it was hard—the tip didn't point down, but struck straight out towards you. His cock was so thick that when he was erect, it didn't get any bigger nor did it rise any higher or wind weird curves; it just stuck straight out at attention as it always did, and got very, very hard. One time, early in our dating days he took off his shorts to fuck me and I said, pointing to his hard (I think) cock, "Aww, look at the little soldier." He didn't look happy but didn't say anything because he was ready to fuck me, but days later, over spaghetti I cooked, I joked again about "the cute little soldier" and he said to me, absolutely soberly, "I don't like that. Please don't say that again." And I didn't, because by that time I was fully in love with him, but I longed to tell him how much I loved the unique smallness of his penis and how it made me love him even more. The feeling of my mouth being filled by a cock that wasn't choking me, and the small, varying undulations of its veins and skin as I wrapped my tongue around it: my little soldier. To me, his cock was like an occult fetish of how perfect we were for each other, because when I sucked it, it felt as though it were molded from the shape of the inside of my mouth, and the inside of my mouth was carved out by the shape of his cock.

One morning about six months into our living together, when I felt he was close, I tried to pry him away from me so I could suck on his balls, which, unlike his cock, were huge. The skin of his ball sac was unusually thick and made the actual testicles seem even bigger. I used to love reaching around to feel his balls tighten and separate as he fucked me in the ass. So that morning I wanted my tongue to feel what my fingers knew. But when I tried to push him out of my mouth, he stopped me. Keeping his hands on the wall, he pushed his hips hard into my face, slamming my head into the headboard of the bed and keeping it there. He stopped moving his hips, because in keeping my head in a vice grip between his crotch and the headboard, he couldn't fuck my mouth properly. So instead, he said: "Keep sucking. And suck until I'm done." He said these words in a voice that felt new. Scott had this great voice, so deep that when he spoke sometimes the words would get caught in his throat. But this voice that felt new was also utterly his regular speaking voice, the one that I was used to: cool, calm, even-keeled. The words he spoke should have been uttered breathlessly, a moment of cheap-porn brought about by the embarrassing self-loss of sexual arousal. Instead, Scott was just himself. I wasn't afraid of him, but my sense of sexiness did die a little bit. I kept sucking until he was done. Without a word, he bounded off the bed to go put the coffee on. I didn't go back to sleep this time. I pulled myself up and sat properly against the headboard and stared off into space. I felt like crying but I was also really hard. I wanted to jerk off but there was a part of me, stronger than that other, which made me wait for my cock to soften. By that time, Scott came back, as he always did, with my morning coffee, its steam softening his hard white face. He handed me my favorite coffee cup: it was made of thick off-white china, in the shape of a cheap diner mug, with two giddy, tiny go-go dancers in stilettos and bustiers, dancing happily with each other. I sipped the hot coffee, and the feeling was the same as it always was: the bitter, flowery coffee mingled with the sweet sour semen of my boyfriend and it all made me feel a little more alive.

"Are you OK?" he asked.

"Yeah."

"OK, good. I didn't want to hurt you. I'm glad."

He gave me a tidy, old-fashioned, smack-loud kiss. Then, looking into my eyes, he kissed me more passionately. After that, I didn't try to move him off me, but every few days, he would push my head back and hold me against the headboard with his unmoving hips.

I was trying to say all this to Val as we walked together on Market Street one weirdly balmy evening. Val never met Scott because I only met her in the last six months or so, and I wanted her to know that Scott wasn't some psychopathic wifebeater rapist jerk. More than that, I wanted her to know that I wasn't on some sad masochist bullshit Billie Holiday nonsense. As cheesy as the words sounded in my own head: "I wasn't a victim. I wanted to be there, I wanted to be with him, I chose to do all these things." Maybe she wouldn't think it was fucked up at all, but judging by the line of her mouth, even in the violet-colored late evening I could tell she thought it was all kinds of fucked up. But I wanted to tell her how this blowjob every morning made me appreciate the morning sky. Mixing cum and coffee in my stomach, I'd stare out the window at the sky as it edged between night and dawn. The sky was so black but at the same time so grey. I wanted to say it was a "blush grey" because I knew dawn was bright, naked red, but truly, the sky after blowjobs was a very dark grey. I learned to become a morning person.

But I didn't tell her all this. When your friend finishes listening to your story of being forced to suck your boyfriend's cock for 300 consecutive mornings and asks, "Did you feel abused?" you can't exactly start talking about the color grey as your explanation for your answer No.

Instead, I just said: "No. I liked it. I admit, sometimes it was uncomfortable, but only physically so. He never acted that way out of bed."

"Does Fei Fei know about this?"

"No. She really hated Scott already. And after we broke up, it seemed pointless to tell her. Also, it wasn't that I was ashamed but . . . it was . . . embarrassing, somehow."

"I think the fact that you felt embarrassed should tell you something. But hey, I don't want to judge. If you say you didn't feel abused, and you enjoyed it, I take your word for it. If you like rough sex . . . well, more power to ya." The words sounded cruel. And although her voice softened the cruelty, Val too felt this and caught herself. "I mean that, I'm not trying to be facetious."

"I understand. I know it sounds fucked up, the way I tell it."

"I guess it's because there's different kinds of violence, you know. You don't have to have bruises or bleed to be hurt, and you don't have to be a housewife to be a victim of domestic abuse."

"I wasn't a victim."

"Yeah, I know. But, was he always violent during sex? You say he wasn't like that out of bed but your just saying that makes me think you knew that in bed, he was acting in a way that wasn't good for you. So out of bed, maybe he was still behaving in a way that wasn't good for you and you just didn't realize it."

"That's possible. But I never felt trapped, or felt like I was in pain. It's true, he did like to be rough during sex. Well, no, not rough, exactly. Just . . . always in control. He did like to force stuff. But I liked it. I thought he was so hot. I think I still do."

"What was he like when you weren't having sex? Was he controlling about stuff?"

"No. I mean, you know, he liked to have his way. I'm pretty sure he came from money, but he was never explicit about that. But I could tell; you don't start your own business in your twenties and not have family money."

"He had his own business?"

I laughed a little. "He had a barbershop. Close to the Pilsner, actually, in that empty space next to Lucky 13? It was called Hops N Heads. He sold local brew in the back of the shop, totally illegally and finally he got busted. He trained as a barber at Joe's Barbershop. Then he started siphoning clients and of course Joe's got mad, rightfully. But Scott was right too; he has a right to have his own business."

"I guess."

"He had a really sweet smile, a little boy kind of smile.

But he talked to people always from a distance. Like they were more than strangers; more like servants."

"To you, too?"

"I don't know. We lived together, did almost everything together so I never felt like that but sometimes, I would catch ourselves in a moment and realize there was that same kind of distance placed against me, too."

I don't know why I was compelled to tell Val about Scott. Maybe because she looked kind of like him tonight. In flesh, they looked nothing alike, but they shared an outline. Also, they had the same color of eyes—engine coolant blue—but Val's eyes were clean, wide, limpid. Scott had small eyes that were almost beady. He smoked a lot of pot, so his eyes were always bloodshot. Because his irises were uncommonly small, the bloodshot made his blue eyes look red, like those of an albino mouse. But I thought that was sexy. The openings of his eyes were sharp, as if the skin over his eyes were cut with a X-Acto knife and pinched open, and his narrow nose and lips, too, looked sharp, carved with another precise blade. Val had her hair back tonight like Scott used to, and she was wearing a plain white t-shirt, which was Scott's uniform. Val's white shirt said "Paula's Pizza" over the heart in pink, green, and purple Day-Glo letters that made me feel a little carsick, and the back was silkscreened with a generic smiley face with a gooey pizza out of its mouth saying "Have a Nice Day," all in the same dizzy colors. Scott tolerated nothing but plain white tees that were thrown out the day they began yellowing in the pits, and always matched with khaki or black work pants, Carhartt or Ben Davis. I think Val's blue work pants were Ben Davis.

We had just come from the SF LGBT Center, where I had gotten my HIV test and it had come back negative, and were walking to the Pilsner for a drink. It wasn't a celebratory drink per se, because although we didn't explicitly talk about it, I felt like we agreed it was in bad taste to associate celebration with HIV status. So it was more of a drink of relief and exhale. I was pretty nervous about the result, and I ought to have been considering how much cum I was allowing Jeb to dump inside me. We had been fucking pretty regularly since we first met, and often drunk and often rubberless. But this particular HIV test was not about Jeb, but had everything to do with Scott—well, everything but Scott's sperm, anyway.

The last Sunday of May this year, I was dancing in *Sleeping Beauty*, which was my last performance for the season. Once again, I was in the wedding party in the last act. Every year I nurse a vague hope that I'll get a featured part—maybe Puss-in-Boots or the Red Riding Hood's Wolf—I know it sounds crazy for those characters to be in *Sleeping Beauty* but that's the ballet. I don't know why I always hope. It's not like I've become any better or more determined. Instead, I'm only older. At least last year I got to be one of the Mazurka dancers; this year, I was partnered up with a girl whose weight was always about to spill over, and both of us grinned our asses off while doing half-assed *pas de deux* in the back of the party, our backs almost touching the painted scrim, both of us knowing that this is where we clearly belonged. The performance was over by 3:30, and I was out of the theatre and on the Market Street trolley by 4:00, my stage makeup barely wiped off, so there were lines of white grease along my hairline, jaw, and neck, globs of black eye pencil still grubbed into my eyebrow hairs. Being part of the wedding party, at least they let me wear my own hair so that looked OK. I felt quite depressed, and wanted to be alone, so I headed up to the Castro and one of the cheesy video dance clubs.

It was a good sign that Fleetwood Mac's "Gypsy" was playing when I came through the doors of the club. I went straight to the basically empty bar lined in gross steel mucked up with fingerprints and asked for a double tequila, then went through to the dance floor. The front of the club, where the bar was, was basic—bricked walls, video screens everywhere, vague benches and bars on stilts. The back dance floor area, at this time of the day, looked like the way a cheap bar would look at night—darkness covering over the patina of human dumbness. The bare dance floor, as silver and mirrored as it were, still looked as brown as lumber from the 1970s, with spit and booze and ashes and tears and blood gathered through four decades. I dropped my backpack in one corner under the three giant video screens, downed half of the tequila, and holding the rest delicately, moved to the center of the floor and started spinning and lip-synching along to Stevie Nicks. "Gypsy" then became "I Don't Know Anybody Else" by Black Box, but it was a strange, really slow version with a lot of strings and no real beat. I'd never heard it before but it really put me in the mood and I let the first half of the tequila irradiate my cells while I moved to it. I took off my jean jacket and, mid-spin, tossed it on top of my backpack and "I Don't Know Anybody Else" became "Crazy For You" by Madonna. I was just going back and forth between swaying and thrashing, all alone, and even through that slow song and some more I was sweating like a pig. Four in the afternoon at a gay dance club meant random music—either old shit for the old alcoholics or random stuff that the VJ liked, although I don't know what this mix was since I think it was actually a pre-set DVD: there was no one in the VJ booth.

My pits and the hollow of my chest was damp with sweat, as was my crotch and the crack of my ass. I was wearing an old white t-shirt, a "Bay to Breakers" shirt with a drawing of a Greek-sandaled foot hovering above a banana peel, and purple-grey sweatpants. I'm sure my sweat stains looked crazy but I didn't care. I finished the rest of my tequila and went back to the bar to get a refill. I was waiting to get the bartender's attention—he was a young cute guy, busy chatting with an old-timer at the other end of the bar—when a guy I didn't know came up to me and asked me if I wanted a drink.

"Sure, thanks," I said. "A double tequila?"

The guy smiled. He was a white guy, tall, nicely built, blond hair that was nearly bald on top but quite thick at the nape of his neck, very tidily trimmed. His eyes and mouth were arranged in such a way, crowded around a quite elegant, very straight sharp nose upon an otherwise generously oval face that he reminded me of a wolf crossed with an anteater; if you squinted he looked sort of like a handsome middle-aged man. I was torn between squinting or not.

"You don't remember me, do you?" the guy said. That didn't bode well, but I wasn't going to pass up a free drink. He had a slightly nasal voice, and he drew out and curled his last syllables. Besides, the arch delicacy of his speaking mixed with his slightly oxen body seemed sexy to me.

"No. Should I?"

"We met once. I'm a friend of Scott's."

The guy turned and waved to the bartender, who came over and took our orders.

I just said, "Oh." Then I averted my eyes and waited for the drink.

"Cheers," the guy lifted up the vodka cranberry he ordered and I smiled weakly and downed my tequila in one gulp. He smiled, showing his pointy teeth and sipped his through his straw; half the glass was empty after two sips.

He heaved a big, smiling sigh and looked at me.

"Another?"

"Sure, why not. Thanks." As he motioned to the bartender, I said, "So, how is Scott these days?"

"He's good. I think he's very happy in Portland."

"Portland?"

"You didn't know?"

I shook my head. Scott and I really didn't have many—any—friends in common, and all of this was before social media. The guy proceeded to tell me that Scott had moved to Portland last month to open a barbershop that was also a café.

I snorted contemptuously as I downed my tequila and my contemptuousness almost sent the tequila into my sinuses. "He's doing that thing again?" I sneered.

"Yeah, he is," the guy said, and I was gratified by his tone of amused resignation. "But he has a really great business partner. Eric used to work at Blue Bottle Coffee." The guy pulled a cellphone out of his pocket, one of those new Apple phones. "Here," he said as he pulled up a photo on the screen of the phone.

Scott was grinning, and next to him was a very young, very pretty black guy, with high cheekbones and dark skin.

"Eric is also his life partner," the guy said.

"*Life* partner?" I snorted even louder, although I didn't know whether I was trying to perform disdain towards this guy or Scott. Scott disliked using even the word "boyfriend" because it made both of us sound too "girly." "Scott went off to start a business and 'life' with a barista?"

"Eric was an executive in Blue Bottle's marketing division," the guy answered, without breaking his smile.

Suddenly I couldn't hear what old or cheesy music was blaring over the speakers; all I could hear was fucking Tchaikovsky, the *Danse Polonaise*, the damn Mazurka music. My head felt like it was going to pieces.

"Would you," I said, "Would you mind terribly getting me another drink? I'll pay you back, I think my wallet is in my backpack over there." I gestured dumbly towards the dance floor, which was, without me on it, totally empty although now more people, less visibly alcoholic, were beginning to stream into the club.

"No worries," the guy said, still smiling, this time smiling directly at my crotch.

You'd have thought that then I proceeded to get fucked up and gone home with this guy. I did get fucked up, but when I woke up the next morning, I wasn't with him. I was in a small bedroom, its whitewashed walls made uncannily whiter by the sun streaming through the window. In the bed next to me, among clean sheets, peach-colored with thin black window pane checks, was a cute young guy in his twenties with curly hair, soft skin and very large, hairy hands. In the corner of the room I saw the red nylon lump of my backpack, and next to that, my purple sweat pants and a patch of a banana on white cotton. I exhaled a big sigh of relief but my head hurt like hell; the last thing I remembered was another double tequila and the guy—the other guy, the messenger, his mouth open and words coming out.

I got out of bed as quietly as I could. I put my clothes on and shook out my hair and stretched vertically, arms straight up, and let my head hang forward. I heard a voice from the bed say hey.

"Hey," I turned and said, trying to match the friendliness of this guy's voice. "It was fun but I really have to go. I left my dog home alone all night." Honestly, I couldn't remember at all if it had been fun or not but I felt horrible about Delilah.

“OK, I understand. Yeah, it was fun.” The guy sat up and arranged himself quite beautifully. I was grateful that he didn’t make a move to get out of bed. “Do you want to hang out again?”

“Yeah, maybe? Let’s exchange numbers.”

The guy reached over to his bedside table and wrote into an expensive-looking leather diary. He tore the page out and held it out for me. I took and unfolded the sheet: Kevin. I wrote my name and number in the diary on his lap.

“OK, catch ya later,” I said cheerfully, although my teeth hurt.

“Hey, wait a minute,” the guy’s voice suddenly sounded a bit sheepish. “I want to let you know there’s a chance I’m HIV positive.”

“What?”

“The last guy I had sex with tested positive last month. I haven’t had a chance to get tested yet. I don’t think you have to worry though,” he said.

“Oh? Why?”

“Well, you know. We didn’t fuck. I didn’t go near your ass.”

“Well, yes, we didn’t have anal sex but you did fuck my mouth,” I said, and because I was blurring, in an extra arch tone.

“Yeah, but I didn’t come in your mouth.”

“Oh, thank you for that and thank you for reminding me. I wish you had told me all of this before we had sex.”

“Why? Would it have made a difference? You know

there's lots of guys out there who will have sex with you and not tell you they're HIV positive. I'm telling you, I'm being honest."

"Oh, you're a prince. You're honest all right, but you have a fucked up sense of timing."

The guy smiled in a way that made his cute face nasty. "Do you even remember how drunk you were when you picked me up at the Powerhouse?"

The Powerhouse was not the bar I was at when I found out about Scott's new life. I didn't have anything to say, and I didn't want to fight with this Kevin person. The way he was speaking was aggressive and defensive, and even in my state I knew that he was mostly correct. But his words, his voice, his smile with his cheek tucked into his neck and cocking his head to one side, it all felt like a big glob of glossy goo, bright, lively but frightening, surging at me; it could have been a warm embrace of silk but just as likely, chewing gum shellacked with saliva and me just a head of tangled hair. I stood there in this other person's room, bright goo coming at me and all of my bad feelings welled up like a different kind of goo, oyster-flesh becoming nacreous, liquid mercury or some other kind of softening metal, spewing out of me and upon contact with this air come to hard horizontal point, pulled like taffy into a point as sharp and hard as a needle, the slipperiness of metal that gum couldn't tangle up.

I shrugged and left, to figure out where the fuck I was so I could get home to Delilah. I hoped I was still in San Francisco but far enough from home not to have to talk to Kevin again. Thankfully, I was.

So now it was almost the end of August, and although three months is the minimum window for HIV antibodies to show up, I couldn't wait any longer: I had marked the date exactly three months from that night with Kevin to go get tested. I don't know why it was having sex with a gay guy who might be HIV positive that made me all antsy about getting an HIV test, when I had spent the last three months letting a guy—Jeb—who may or may not be bisexual—pour his semen into both ends of me. I worried that it was internalized homophobia, but I couldn't allow myself to think too much about that.

I called to ask Fei Fei if she would come with me for the HIV test. She answered, but she was in Washington, near Spokane on a big buying tour and wouldn't be back until next week. She suggested I call up Val.

"She has a lot of experience with that sort of thing. I think she'd be really comforting," she said.

After I signed in at the front desk, Val and I sat down in the waiting room, on soft nubby grey chairs, the walls painted in the soft-boiled egg yellow and hot violet. Val and I both noted that coming softly from speakers overhead was Cassandra Wilson's "You Don't Know What Love Is."

"What a weird choice for an AIDS clinic," Val said. "Good, but weird." Her voice made me see sheets of thick, clean blank paper being stacked, one by one. I felt safe.

"Yeah, it is weird but good," I said. And we listened silently together to the rest of the song. We assumed the radio had been tuned into KCSM 91.1, but after the song ended it went right into Cassandra singing "Come On In My Kitchen."

"They're playing the whole *Blue Light 'Til Dawn* album," I said.

"Yeah, they are. Weird!" said Val.

0o0

I DON'T KNOW ABOUT JAMIE, BUT I WAS EXHAUSTED, as if we had been walking the whole night through, forced to walk, fleeing from a definite but faceless danger, when in fact we had only been talking. Talking, talking endlessly, endlessly about us: I don't know that I wouldn't have preferred walking all night. We began around 5 p.m., as we were getting ready to go out to dinner. Reservations were canceled, hunger forgotten. Instead, I smoked some cigarettes and we finished a half bottle of gin. When we started we were both standing: Jamie was leaning against the door, unforgiving and unbending, me putting my pants on. Then we both sat on the bed facing each other for a long time, and when I began to cry, Delilah acted the emotional support animal and jumped up to literally lick my tears away. Her tongue is big and heavy, so it nearly knocked me over, and her peach-pit skull shape revealed as her big triangle ears pulled back, sad flags in the wind. Jamie and I talked into dawn, and when we were too exhausted with all our words, we just put our foreheads together, took each other's clothes off and jacked each other off, laying on our sides, face to face, eyes open, mouths turned down. Then we were able to sleep for a couple hours.

I really hadn't intended to break up with Jamie last night. First off, I didn't think there was anything to "break up" because we had never said we were in a relationship—we had never even decided to be exclusive with one another. But I also decided I couldn't let things go in that direction any more, which meant I couldn't let him come see me every time he was in town, I couldn't go up weekends to see him, I couldn't have sex with him every time we saw each other, I couldn't complain to him about stuff going on with my friends or my depression about work, I couldn't let myself ponder thoughts of how his HIV status could evolve and when it might actually ravage him, I couldn't let him buy me dinner every time we saw each other, I couldn't accept gifts from him (like the stunning silver bracelet in the shape of a sunburst, its zig-zag edges jabbing softly into my wrist, its metal heaviness a campy kind of cradling, its joint clicking like a lock when I put it on, as if it were made for me, even though it wasn't, it was made almost sixty years ago by a famous Mexican silversmith named Antonio Pineda, and Jamie bought it for me at an antique jewelry shop in Healdsburg even though it cost $1400 and I protested, albeit half-heartedly), I couldn't let us keep talking together about our respective pasts and let them entwine into mutuality like decorative ruby-eyed snakes around our wrists (another bracelet, another shop). I couldn't do all those things and in the commas between those moments fuck Jeb and let myself fall in love with him—Jeb, I mean.

I didn't verbalize any of these things to Jamie, nor did I plan to, probably ever. I almost told him about Jeb, but when I rolled Jeb's name in my mouth it felt stupid. Nevertheless, around 10 p.m. I decided to just say it anyway.

"What if I meet someone I fall in love with? What if you meet someone you fall in love with?" I asked.

"I'm in love with you, Howie."

"I know you said that, I know you think that. But what if suddenly we find that someone we're just casually fucking becomes that person we fall in love with?"

"Well, that happened to me," he said. I was silent. After a moment, he asked, "Have *you* fallen in love with someone else?"

In the end, I decided to lie. "No," I said. "I'm just talking hypothetically. I mean, it could happen to you."

"I'm not fucking anyone else but you."

"But we never talked about that! I never asked you to be monogamous and I don't expect you to!"

"I know you don't. It was my choice."

I was fuzzy with frustration because I truly hadn't planned on breaking up with Jamie; I was intending to do it the coward's way, over the phone, sometime next week in that future when it is always "sometime next week." Instead, now we were in his car both of us alert and woozy from lack of sleep, following Fei Fei's car at 8 a.m. on our way to hang out with some redwood trees in Oakland for her birthday celebration hike. We were both still and wordless as Jamie drove and I sat to the right, the cool burgundy leather puff of the BMW interior feeling much more comforting than my bed, those tangled sheets speckled with sweat, tears, and sperm. I leaned back into the seat and tilted the vents so they shot the cool air directly into my face, and set my interior temperature at 65 degrees even though Jamie had his at 70, hoping I could be cured of all my gross moist sadness and anxiety. Fei Fei's birthday gift sat in the backseat, as cold and cool as I wished I were, in a box, with glossy white paper wrapping, with chic narrow white satin ribbon bow, cardboard box as thick as slim wood planes, snowy tissue paper layered and folded as if complex origami: an expensive white blouse from the Anne Fontaine shop downtown, with sharp, large clerical collars that were layered thickly and repeated as long cuffs, tiny white covered buttons there and all down the front. The gift was to be from both Jamie and me, us, and I could feel it grow increasingly uneasy in spite of its coolness. Directly behind me sat Delilah, next to the gift, and in the rearview mirror I could see her eyes trained on me in a rare mood of uncertainty; rather than resting her chin on her crossed paws, she kept her neck taut for the entire drive, a pink-tongued watchtower.

Driving together in silence felt like such a cliché to me, and the absurdity of the tension was starting to make me irritated. I turned on the stereo and a blast of electronic maracas hit us mid-song. I recognized it as a tribal house-style remix of a song by this band from the '70s, famous for their cutesy frontwoman and songs that shellacked gross punk attitude into glossy disco-pop. They hadn't made a record together for decades and this song was a reunion tune, even though now it was itself a couple years old. I liked it, even in its club mix but to me it just sounded like the frontwoman's solo stuff from the '90s. The car stereo caught the song right as the bells and beats gave way to the pleading chorus, which was the name of a girl, although not the name of the frontwoman herself.

"I didn't know you liked them. I didn't know you liked this song," I said as coldly as possible but I'm pretty sure it sounded a bit pleading.

"I don't," Jamie answered without turning his head. "It's just on a mix that a friend made for me."

"Well, I like it."

It was a very long version of the song and by the time it was fading out we were at our destination. We parked next to Fei Fei and everyone piled out like clowns from a clown car. Fei Fei's car was a veritable caravan that held Fei Fei and Val, who were now starting to date again, a tentative second try; Jean and her new girlfriend, a tall, buxom Swede named Ingrid, who had her presumably Scandinavian blond hair dyed powder-red and was wearing an improbable outfit of hiking boots, stretchy black striped leggings, a tight red cardigan with pearl buttons with just the bottom two fastened so that it revealed a black strapless scallop-edged bra; Tish and her new girlfriend Lou, a thin, strong-looking Jewish girl with big, spongy hair; and Kala, in from L.A. and the only one who wasn't paired off, and looking quite pleased about it.

Loaded with our picnic baskets and coolers, we started out of the parking area and into the park proper. This particular parking area—for I think there must have been several, for the several entrances to the park—was an unceremonious patch of pale dust. As there was no pavement, there were no grids for the cars, so our cars just staked out our own little shape away from the three cars that were already there: a shiny new pickup truck parked next to a beat-up old station wagon, and a neat little red compact parked by itself near the entrance sign. The parking area was the oblong oval shape of a bean, with the convex side butting up against the highway and the concave side just sloping off into a soft kind of valley. That edge of the parking lot had no guardrails or even ropes and posts, but led directly down to a drop that must have been at least ten feet. But I suppose it wasn't too dangerous because the drop was sloped in the same beige dirt of the parking lot and led gently down to the bottom of the valley, which reminded me of a drained pool, but not at all sad like drained pools. It was a vast area, huge and extending to distant forests, whose green life emphasized how dead the bottom of the valley actually was: all beige and grey, dust rising quietly into the air from a ground dotted with rocks and thin, elfin desiccated brushes that looked as if they were twigs pushed into the ground by happy kids. To me it all felt optimistic in a weird sort of way because the parking area itself seemed to blur and smudge into nature itself. But nature wasn't ripe fruits and moist green leaves but the dust of stones, tree bark, and bones, mistaken for seeds or pollen by someone as desperate as I was. I felt the way I did when I used to walk up to Grace Cathedral late at night, alone, and sit in the middle of the stone maze. This was almost a decade ago, when I first moved to San Francisco, and I was crashing with four other dancers in a walk-up on Leavenworth Street. I was so depressed then, the only thing that would flatten that feeling was to sit in that place and look around at the night-darkened stone church, and into the rectangular quads at the dim glow in the windows of the cloisters, imagining monks studying. I don't believe in god, but this was something like a prayer, I suppose.

We had to walk along the edge of the concave side of the parking lot in order to get on the hiking path, which was in fact just another edge of this pale valley. Because the path was quite narrow, we all had to fall into little clumps of twos. Fei Fei and Val were marching like professionals far in the front, Val with a giant red mountain-pack worn like a papoose, and Fei Fei already having picked up a witchy hiking stick. I heard her cry out: "I said no talking about politics today! I'm so tired of talking about stuff that we all agree on!" Then Val's good-natured laughter. Tish and Lou were next, all lovey-dovey. Lou seemed exactly like the kind of girl Tish always went for, which is to say not butch but only because she had long hair. Lou had a body similar to mine, thin and long-waisted, and was kind of dressed like me too, although her clothes looked tougher, almost metallic. I was wearing an old purple Righteous Babe Records shirt with these pants made out of striped denim, black with very pale red, very thin vertical lines woven into the fabric, like OshKosh jeans from childhood, complete with four pockets including a pair of patch back pockets, except the front pockets were slashed, not comfy curved, and it closed with a hook and eye and the three buttons for the fly were of soft wood. I didn't have any hiking boots so I just wore my running shoes. Everyone had on proper hiking boots except me and Lou, who was wearing faded black Chucks.

Jamie was going along with Jean and Ingrid, falling back sometimes when the path became too narrow, moving forward with Jean when Ingrid stopped to stare off round into space. I could tell that he was in intermittent but intense conversation with Jean, and it made me feel like shit. Jamie had bought a beautiful, complete hiking outfit at REI—he even signed up for their co-op membership. His hiking boots were soft brown suede with purple mesh and sea-foam green patent leather trimmings, with solid toothed gripper soles of strong Vibram rubber, brown with white specks. Then, too, a black nylon, moisture-wicking mock turtle-neck t-shirt and narrow (but not tight) hiking pants made of thicker black nylon with subtle cargo pockets, and a black Patagonia fleece vest with a nipped-in waist. The vest finished off the whole look, made him look as if he weren't the nature dilettante he and I actually were, but he had to leave the vest in the car because this morning was bizarrely hot. August is always hot in the Bay

Area but mornings are usually never hot. This morning was so hot that the day seemed to belong to some other place and time altogether. Rearing up the very tail of the party with Delilah and Kala, I watched Jamie from about ten feet back. He seemed younger than he usually looked. Not that he looked old usually, but today his body had the wobbliness and energy of a teenager. He looked narrower and more vulnerable, and without the vest, a bit melancholic.

I felt my little cell phone buzz in my left back pocket. I flicked my cigarette butt into the valley to get the phone out. It was an SMS message from Jeb: "dreamed of fuckin u raw last nite cdlnt sleep. jerked off thinking abt u fucked."

"Oh brother," I blurted out, as much at Jeb's dumb message as for my own dumb penis, tingling in spite of everything.

"You shouldn't litter, Howie," Kala drawled ironically as she dropped her cigarette butt on the path and ground it out. She was the only one of the party wearing sunglasses that blocked her eyes out completely: big black plastic wraparounds. She asked, with obvious fake innocence, "What's going on with you? Are you and Jamie not getting along?"

I sighed. "Jamie and I are not a thing, so there is no 'getting along' or 'not getting along,' you know?"

"OK, but it doesn't seem that way to me. That's not what Jean says, anyway. But you know best," Kala's words hurt me a little, but as always, the dreamy rhythm and scratchy tone of her speaking gave me a feeling of comfort.

"Well, what does Jean say?" I asked. Kala shrugged and said in her words what I knew had been happening between me and Jamie—that we were not "dating" but Jamie felt as though we basically were.

"He's unhappy," Kala said.

"But that's not fair. We never agreed to be in a relationship, in fact, *in point of fact,* I explicitly told him I wasn't ready for a relationship. And I'm not! I think it's so unfair how everyone presumes to know me better than my own self!"

"I'm pretty sure Jean didn't say that Jamie wanted you to agree to be his boyfriend. I think he fully understands that you don't want to be in a relationship, period. We all get that. What Jean said is exactly what I just told you: Jamie *feels* unhappy. He's just really sad."

Kala's word "unhappy" buzzed in my brain. I stared down at our three sets of feet. There was so much dust, but it didn't feel grimy, like when people said dust to mean dirt, as in dirty, not dirt as in earth. This must have been dust (dirt) from bones of dead animals or ancient minerals. But I kept thinking instead about decimated concrete and face powder from glossy black enamel compacts. Those grains must also be dust, in some way? On the path the dirt wasn't all just beige as it was in the parking lot; rather, it was green, rose, and grey, all mixed together, separable only in the clarity of the harsh early morning California sun that burned through everything. What's for sure is that the rose-colored dust really did belong in a Chanel compact. The black toenails of Delilah emerging from her golden foot-fur were coated with the pale dust but it looked beautiful, especially next to our stupid human shoes, on which it truly looked just like dirt in the grossest sense.

"Kala," I pleaded, "You of all people should know. Don't you think we have the right to be as deeply intimate as someone as we want to without . . . moving in with them, sharing rent and grocery bills, planning retirement together, all that shit."

"Yeah, I do, I do know," she answered in her slow-paced voice. "I've always felt like lovers make a woman messy, slovenly, even. I like feeling alone and clean. But then again, sometimes messy is good."

I looked down at our feet again, not able to look Kala in the eye. The pebbles here were square—or rather, cubic, as if they were cut for elaborate platinum claw-settings. The grey, green, and rose of the dirt was also in these tough-looking pebbles strewn about, except there were more of the rose-colored ones and their color seemed to deepen into an almost brick-red the more we walked on. I kicked one and raised pinkish green dust.

"But it seems unfair that I should be blamed for Jamie's unhappiness just because I want to remain clean, like you," I said.

"But I wouldn't assume his unhappiness is all about you," said Kala.

Up ahead Jamie was crying. We were too far back to see actual tears, although I'm almost sure I saw sparkles on his cheeks make tiny blinding bursts of light. He was crying with his whole body, shoulders pressing into his sternum, jackhammer convulsions as he pressed his head into Jean's shoulder.

Suddenly, Delilah bolted from our side, and in puffs of green, grey, and rose, ran straight to Jamie and leapt upon him, her proportionally delicate but actually huge paws tamping his stomach, her big neck stretched out, long pink tongue darting and longing towards his face.

"Delilah! Stop, girl!" I cried out, and Kala and I both kind of trotted quickly to catch up to Jean, Jamie, and Delilah, Ingrid having walked ahead by herself. I pulled Delilah down from Jamie, whose immaculate black clothes were covered with dirt, dust, and dog hair. I made Delilah sit, but as soon as she put her butt on the ground she sprang up again and began a high-pitch whine that I rarely, if ever, heard from her. She began to lunge at Jamie again, and it was obvious it was not a lunge of aggression, even if she had made small claw-slashes on Jamie's arms, red raised lines dotted with blood droplets.

"I'm sorry, I don't know what has gotten into her. She never does this, usually," I said, mainly to Jamie but also vaguely at Jean and Kala.

"It's OK," Jamie replied. Eyes red and cheeks wet, he squatted down and let Delilah lick away his tears; she licked with crazy abandon and obsessiveness. "Look, can we talk a little, Howie? By ourselves?" he asked while looking into Delilah's focused eyes.

Kala took the leash from my hand and said, "We'll take girl on ahead. You know I walk slow so you guys can catch up easily with us."

Jean nodded in agreement and the three of them began walking on. I turned to Jamie.

"I just don't know if I can talk any more, Jamie," I said, totally defeated. Jamie, too, looked defeated, and weirdly this made me feel closer to him in a way I hadn't felt before. Still he didn't look at me; instead he was looking round to the right at some trees. He took my hand and began to walk towards the trees, and the phone buzzed in my pocket again.

We walked hand-in-hand off the path into a small kind of landing where the dirt was darker—just slightly, auburn. It seemed to be the outer edge of a forest. The trees that Jamie had been staring at were suddenly all upon us, shockingly tall, frail but dark and definitive, thin black lines that seemed to block out the top of the sky altogether, and joined to the brown-grey ground, made us feel as though we were floating: there was no difference between earth and sky. Because the trees were so thin you could see snatches of the perfectly blue sky, but because there were so many trees, the sky was merely imitating the slim black trees, thin blue laths. All around were green leaves—I have no idea what kind of trees these were—were they the redwoods? The sun sieved its light through the leaves and cast beautiful shadows on the ground, a carpet of fancy black lace.

Originally, Fei Fei had talked about doing this birthday party on the beach, at night. Not Stinson Beach, certainly not Baker Beach, but perhaps Ocean Beach. But then Val told her about a film that contained a scene of frolicking young lesbians on a beach at night and that totally turned Fei Fei off, of which I'm glad because I don't like beaches at night. In fact, I don't really at all like the beaches of the Bay Area; they remind me of beaches in winter. A beach in winter: everything is blue-grey like the sea, even the sand. The sea refuses to melt and it's as if, rather, the atmosphere gives in to the temperature of the sea's interior, the interior that is so cold yet not freezing, a cold that instead petrifies, houses in blue amber, pulsing warm-blooded bodies. The beaches in Northern California are like that, perpetual beaches in winter. I was thankful for the cool gold light of the sun and the thin black trees.

Jamie led me further towards the trees. The ground sloped here and there, and I felt a little like an undulating slalom. We walked between the trees towards a soft ledge lined with bursts of wild golden-green bushes with thin, spiky leaves. From there we could finally see the horizon proper, where the sky turned into a white line against the tops of the trees.

We looked out for a long time, holding hands. Then I pulled him away.

"Let's catch up with the others," I said.

Jamie nodded and we started walking back to the path. But amid the trees he stopped, and turned to face me, his mouth open, expectantly.

"No," I said before any words could come out of his mouth. "Really. I just can't talk any more. I don't have anything more to say, I can't find anything more to say."

"Then just fuck me," Jamie replied. He said this without anger or resentment, just simply as if he were commenting on the weather. He pulled me towards him, and backed himself against a tree. He began to kiss me and I leaned into it. He pulled his pants down and the slippery nylon fell easily round his ankles. He struggled more with my pants, but they, too, eventually fell and he began jerking my cock, which was already semi-hard. I reached over and rubbed his cockhead until I felt the precum. I think he was moaning but I'm not sure with the insects and leaves and branches and rocks all buzzing all around us. I really wanted to fuck him. Jamie spat into his palm and calmly jerked me. With his other hand, he guided my hand into the warm, fuzzy place between his asscheeks, cushiony with hair. This excited me.

"Just fuck me," he repeated.

"But I don't have any condoms," I said, sounding and feeling dumb.

"Just do it," he said.

Pushing him into the tree. I turned my hips this way and that, moving my cockhead around his butthole, vibrating against the damp hard curls there. I could feel Jamie's soft opening but I rubbed more against the curls; it felt great. Finally, I popped my cockhead into his anus and pushed in with a rough thrust.

It was hard to fuck standing, against a thin tree. We didn't quite know what to do with our pant-hobbled legs, and a part of me felt like we were both trying to be careful not to hurt the thin tree, even though I'm pretty sure that the thin tree could have withstood the weight and force of much more than two lame fags. I tried to lift Jamie's butt a bit with my hands but that seemed impossible. Jamie spread his legs as wide as he could given the circumstances, and I felt a sharp, triangular bone through the flesh of his ass; I imagined his butt forming a sharp "W" shape as I fucked him. When I was close I started to pull out, but Jamie grabbed my butt and held it still, and I realized I was much closer than I had calculated: I felt my legs stiffen almost into a Charlie horse as I shot my load inside him. It felt great, but also supremely shitty.

"Oh fuck," I said over and over as I pressed into Jamie's whole body. I hugged him, and he held me back, hard. Between Oh Fucks I kept apologizing, and he kept saying it was OK. It didn't feel OK but it was all done.

When my cock softened out from his rectum, we pulled our pants up, neither of us bothering or caring to wipe any stuff off us. We zipped and buttoned up and walked out from between the trees.

"I'm getting a little cold," Jamie said. "I want to go back to the car and get my vest. Will you come with me?" He asked as if we were at a cotillion and the waltz was striking up. *Blue Danube*.

"Yup, let's go," I said.

We got back on the path, back towards the parking area. A tiny little creature—a salamander?—just a shade greener than the dirt flitted across the path in front of us. The sun seemed suddenly higher up and the ground looked brighter, whiter, almost like the unfinished marble of a museum or a distant acropolis.

Jamie had stopped so as to not step on the salamander, and he walked over to a sign on the side of the path we hadn't noticed earlier. It was placed at the very edge of a path, obscured by some brushes. A large placard, encased in a metal frame welded to a strong metal pole driven into the ground, showed an illustrated sort of information, faded teal color, with images of mammoths and antelopes and flowers, under Plexiglas that was very old, cracked and stained, and there were bits of dirt, dead insects and foliage caught between.

I stood next to Jamie in front of the sign and read out loud, my voice still hoarse from talking so much the night before: "'Prior to European settlement, California's grasslands were dominated by wildflowers and perennial, asterisk, bunchgrasses, rather than the exotic annual grasses that outcompete our native flora today. The serpentine prairie before you is a small remnant of the native grassland that once supported herds of prehistoric horses, bison, camels, mammoths, and more recently, elk.'" Jamie still looked ahead, not looking at me, but eyes soft. I continued, "And there's a footnote with the asterisk, and that says: 'A perennial plant lives for at least three years. Annual plants live for one growing season and then go to seed.' What does going to seed mean?"

I pictured showgirl legs of bees hairy and sticky with honey, thick petals, silver punk frizzes of flying dandelion heads, the whole world bombed out in pollen, history-whitened wooden telephone poles gone native with moss and vines and buds clinging. Jamie told me what "going to seed" meant. I'm pretty sure I liked my meaning better.

ACKNOWLEDGMENTS

Thank you to...

Everyone at Nightboat: Stephen Motika, Lindsey Boldt, Emily Bark Brown, Lina Bergamini, Lucia Kan-Sperling, Kit Schluter, and especially Dante Silva for his acuity and empathy.

Andrea Lawlor and Nate Lippens for the comradeship and Kye Christensen-Knowles for the beautiful cover painting.

My companion species: Sami and extra kisses to Nella for her patience.

My family: Meenha Lee, Jeung Kang, Tracy Steepy.

My other half Roddy Schrock: without you I'm nothing.

JOON OLUCHI LEE lives and writes in femininity and feminism. He is the author of *Neotenica* (Nightboat Books, 2020), which won the Lambda Literary Award for Gay Fiction. Also the author of *94* (2015) and *Lace Sick Bag* (2013), as well as various essays on queer theory, feminism, and fiction writing, he is Professor in Literary Arts & Studies at Rhode Island School of Design, and, with his partner Roddy, co-parent of their rescue dogs Nella and Sami.

NIGHTBOAT BOOKS

Nightboat Books, a nonprofit organization, seeks to develop audiences for writers whose work resists convention and transcends boundaries. We publish books rich with poignancy, intelligence, and risk. Please visit nightboat.org to learn about our titles and how you can support our future publications.

The following individuals have supported the publication of this book. We thank them for their generosity and commitment to the mission of Nightboat Books:

Kazim Ali, Anonymous (4), Ava Aviva Avnisan, Wilson Baldridge, Jean C. Ballantyne, Rumeli Banik, Will Blythe, Nick Buffon, Rob Byrnes, Martha Chowning & Jonathan Groff, V. Shannon Clyne, Juliana Cobb, Theodore Cornwell, Gisela Gamper, Photios Giovanis, Janlori Goldman, Amanda Greenberger, David Groff & Clay Williams, Daniel Handler, Sarah Heller, Karen Holtzman, Parag Rajendra Khandhar, Shari Leinwand, Elizabeth Madans, Bruno Franco Medeiros, Pooja Mehta, Ethan Mitchell, Caren Motika, Elizabeth Motika, Zehra N, Asker Saeed, Mark Sexton & Kirk Wallace, The Leslie Scalapino - O Books Fund, Amy Scholder, Chloe Silverman, Eric Suchyta, James Voorhies, Jerrie Whitfield & Richard Motika

This book is supported, in part, by a grant from the Poetry Foundation, in addition to public funds from the New York City Department of Cultural Affairs in partnership with the City Council, and the New York State Council on the Arts with the support of the Office of the Governor and the New York State Legislature.

POETRY FOUNDATION NYC Cultural Affairs NEW YORK STATE OF OPPORTUNITY. Council on the Arts

CUANDO LOS MUERTOS HABLAN

Mensajes y experiencias con seres del más allá

Colección
Círculo de Terror